Angel's Mother's Wedding

Other Books by Judy Delton

Kitty from the Start
Kitty in the Middle
Kitty in the Summer
Kitty in High School

Only Jody
Mystery of the Haunted Cabin

Back Yard Angel
Angel in Charge
Angel's Mother's Boyfriend

Angel's Mother's Wedding

Judy Delton

Illustrated by Margot Apple

Houghton Mifflin Company
Boston 1987

Library of Congress Cataloging-in-Publication Data

Delton, Judy.
  Angel's mother's wedding.

  Summary: Angel is worried because her
mother does not seem to be making any preparations for her upcoming wedding.
  [1. Weddings — Fiction.   2. Worry — Fiction.
3. Family life — Fiction]   I. Apple, Margot,
ill.   II. Title.
PZ7.D388Aq   1987   [Fic]   87-16937
ISBN 0-395-44470-5

Printed in the United States of America

P   10   9   8   7   6   5   4   3   2   1

For Patty Lu Pyne from the one who poured at the wedding

Contents

Angel's Mother's Wedding

1.
Angel Makes a List

Angel sat on the back steps of her big green house, thinking about all of the changes that had come about in her life in the last few months. Not long ago she had sat here worrying about little things, like having friends, and her mother's vacation. Now there were big things in her life — her mother was in love with a clown and was going to marry him. That meant that Angel and her small brother Rags would have a clown for a father. For ten years Angel and Rags and their mother had lived quietly in an old house in a small Wisconsin town and hardly anything had happened to change the routine. Then Rudy came, and things had not been quiet since.

Angel had to admit that she was glad that Rudy had come. All of them were happier than they had been before. If Angel even felt a little bit sad, all Rudy had to do was walk into the room with Rags on his shoulders and a big loving smile on his face, and the whole room seemed to light up and it felt like a party was about to begin. Rudy could do that. He could turn any day into a party day.

A few feet from where Angel was sitting on the back steps, a shower of black dirt flew through the air. It came from under the porch. Rags had made an entire small city beneath the house, complete with roads and houses and filling stations and trees and even the Grand Canyon. He had recently added a swimming pool (with real water) and Angel's discarded dolls for citizens. People took his word for this, since the space to crawl into the city was too small for anyone larger than Rags. Rags was just barely five years old and very small. His mother had recently ordered him to stop digging deeper or the house would topple over some night when they were all asleep, and so Rags was expanding his city toward the back yard. His mother called it branching out, and she worried less about the house.

Down the street, Angel caught a glimpse of her friend Edna, who was coming toward Angel's house, on her bike.

"Whoa!" she called to her bike, which she was pretending was a horse. Both Edna and Angel thought it would be fun to have a horse to ride, but since there was no place to keep one (and their mothers would probably object even if there were) they often pretended. Angel and Rags were good at pretending. Their mother said they were very creative. Angel thought it must be very boring not to be creative — there simply was not enough excitement in a small Wisconsin town if you could not invent things.

Hitching her horse to the gatepost with a piece of rope, Edna fed it some imaginary hay. Then she walked up the steps of the back porch and sat down beside Angel.

"I can't wait till school's out," she said.

Angel nodded. "Pretty soon it will be," she said. "And we can do whatever we want all summer long."

"It will be warm," Edna mused. "And we can go to the pool."

"We won't have homework," added Angel, "and we can stay up late."

"And there'll be a wedding!" said Rags, popping his head from under the porch like a jack-in-the-box.

"You aren't supposed to eavesdrop," said Angel crossly.

"What's 'eavesdrop'?" said Rags.

The girls did not pay any attention to him. Sometimes they felt very generous and played with Rags and even took him with them on their adventures. And sometimes they acted as if he didn't exist (Mrs. O'Leary said).

"When *is* the wedding?" asked Edna.

Angel shrugged her shoulders in reply. "We don't know the date yet. But sometime this summer. Probably August."

Edna looked thoughtful. "What are you going to give your mom and Rudy for a wedding gift?" she asked.

"A wedding gift?" said Angel, in surprise.

"A present?" said Rags, his shovel in his hand.

"Well of course," said Edna. "The most important thing about weddings is a wedding gift. I never heard of a wedding where they didn't get presents, did you?"

"No," said Angel, thinking of the few weddings she had seen. People always arrived carrying large boxes with bows and streamers on them, and the paper had bells and brides and lace and things on it. Edna was right: people all brought presents.

Before Angel's head could stop reeling with wedding-present thoughts, Edna said, "Who is going to be the bridesmaid?"

"Bridesmaid?" echoed Angel.

"People have attendants in weddings," Edna went on. "You know, flower girls and a ring bearer and a best man and stuff."

Edna was right again. Weddings were not just the bride and groom. Weddings were like big parties, with people in fancy dress and carrying flowers and with organ music playing. No, it would not just be her mother and Rudy, with Angel and Rags watching the ceremony. There would be crowds of people there to celebrate.

"And there will have to be a reception," Edna went on. "Lots of food for all the guests. You'll need a wedding cake, a real big one, so there's enough for everyone and some to take home to put under your pillow.''

Angel sighed. She had no idea weddings could be so involved. She wondered if her mother had thought about all of this. Maybe she didn't know what she was in for. Maybe she thought (as Angel had) that it was easy to get married.

''It's not too early to think of making plans,'' said Edna. ''One of my aunts got married and she ordered invitations six months ahead of time.''

Six months! August was less than six months away! Maybe she, Angel, should get started writing out the invitations. There was no time to lose.

''What do you say on invitations?'' Angel asked.

''You have to have them printed,'' said Edna, knowledgeably. ''The printer writes something like, 'We request the honor of your presence at the wedding of Mrs. O'Leary and Rudy.' Then they say RSVP at the end.''

''What's it mean, arsveepee?'' said Rags, popping his head over the edge of the porch floor again.

"It means to let them know if they can come or not," said Edna. "You have to know how much food to order. Then of course you have to hire a photographer to take pictures," she went on. "What would a wedding be without pictures?"

"Rudy has a camera," said Rags. "I saw it."

Edna looked disgusted. "Wedding pictures have to be taken by a professional," she said. "They know how to make people smile, and get wrinkles out of their clothes, and they do things like tie a ribbon on the knife when they cut the cake. You can't just cut the cake with an ordinary knife, you know."

Angel and Rags didn't know. They knew very little, it appeared. It should be Edna's mother who was getting married. But then of course she was already married to Edna's father.

Angel wondered why Edna knew so much more than she did. It wasn't just weddings; it seemed to be everything. When Angel had worried that the tax men from Washington were after her mother, Edna seemed to know everything about

Washington and the government and the law.

And when they had opened a dog laundry Edna knew how to advertise and get customers, and even how to please them once they got them. Angel felt cross with her mother now for having sheltered her so. Why, she was a regular social misfit! She and Rags had never heard of RSVP. It was time they got out into the world.

It was up to Angel to learn what to do at a wedding, and to learn it quickly.

At times like this, when Things to Do seemed overwhelming, there was only one thing to do, Angel knew.

"You better make a list," said Edna.

Angel went into the house and got her notebook and a pencil. She came back out and wrote a list, with a large space after each entry:

1. Wedding presents. ???
2. Bridesmaids. ???
3. Food. ???
4. Pictures. ???

She felt a little better after she had listed ten things that had to be planned, but the question marks after each of them bothered her. Her mother had a lot on her mind — her job and her family and her dates with Rudy and her help with his television show. She could not be expected to think of all these wedding things as well, and besides, Angel was sure that she was not aware that so much had to be done. If she was, she would have begun to plan long ago, and she would have mentioned it all to them, and to Rudy. But she hadn't. She just went on smiling and cooking and humming in the kitchen with that pleased look on her face. Poor Mom! Angel didn't have the heart to tell her that a wedding was *work*. That there was trauma ahead. No, she and Rags would bravely bear the brunt of it. They would square their shoulders and make wedding plans and make sure that their mother would not be in an embarrassing position in August.

Angel wrote away, filling page after page in her notebook. Then she frowned and erased and wrote some more. Rags just sat and looked worried and sad.

Edna, who had come over to her friend's house

looking for some amusement, was disappointed. Both Rags and Angel appeared to be in bad moods. There didn't seem to be any fun ahead today. So Edna unhitched her horse from the post, mounted him, and said, "Good-bye" and "Giddap!" and rode off down Kilbourn Avenue.

Angel wrote, "14. Wedding cake. ???" She didn't notice that Edna had gone.

2.
Parade Plans

While Angel was still sitting on the steps brooding over her list, Rudy pulled up to the curb in his car. He was whistling, and when Rags heard him, he left his city and ran to meet him.

"What's new, pal?" said Rudy, swinging Rags up in the air and onto his shoulders.

"People bring presents to weddings," said Rags.

"Ho, that's not new," said Rudy, walking up the steps with Rags on his shoulders. "People have been bringing presents to weddings for years and years."

So Rudy did know something about weddings after all. Angel felt a small surge of relief. Even if their mother was not knowledgeable, Rudy could help.

Rudy sat down beside Angel on the step.

"You will get lots of presents," said Rags. "This many," he added, making an imaginary stack with his hands.

"Well, I know one thing I'll ask my fairy godmother for," said Rudy. "She can give me a new car for a wedding present."

The three of them looked at Rudy's car parked at the curb. It looked a little bit rusty. There were a few dents here and there, and the antenna was bent.

"Actually, this one runs fine," he said. "It probably just needs a coat of paint and it would look like new."

"Do people get cars for wedding presents?" asked Angel. She was sure her allowance would not be enough to buy something like a car. Even an old one.

Rudy laughed. "Only if they have a fairy godmother," he said.

After Rudy went into the house, Angel said,

"It's too bad we can't get Mom and Rudy a car for a wedding present."

"Maybe we could have a dog laundry again," said Rags.

"Rags, cars cost *thousands* of dollars! Not just a hundred."

Rags thought about that. Rudy did say that all his car needed was a coat of paint. Paint was not very expensive. Rags could surely afford to buy a can of paint. He and Angel could surprise Rudy! They could paint the car for him! Or maybe this should be Rags's present alone. He did not need Angel. Angel could get her own present. He had found a wedding present that he could afford! It felt warm and good to have this secret deep inside. And it would be a big surprise as well. Secrets and surprises. Rags loved them both. He must remember not to tell anyone.

When Angel and Rags went into the house, their mother and Rudy were talking. But they were not talking about wedding plans. They were talking about the Memorial Day Parade.

"It will be here before you know it," said Rudy. "And I want to have the best float there."

"Float?" said Angel and Rags together.

"We are all going to ride on it!" said Rudy. "First we have to build it, though," he added. "The TV station will pay for the materials, but we have to put it together."

Rudy had an afternoon television show for children. It was so successful that the station had had to give him a larger studio.

It seemed to Angel that Rudy and her mother should be making wedding plans, not parade plans. But the more Rudy talked, the more exciting the parade sounded. Rudy could do that — make a person forget one thing and get excited about something else brand new.

Until this year, Angel and Rags and their mother had only been spectators at the Memorial Day parades. This would be the first time they would be *in* one! That surely felt like something to get excited about!

Rudy was already getting paper and pencils

and crayons out on the dining room table.

"Now!" he said. "What should our float look like?"

Rags began to jump up and down. "Like a boat?" he said. "Boat, float!" Rags was good at rhyming things.

"Not a boat," said Angel, disgusted with Rags's snap decisions. He always said whatever came into his head, with no time spent thinking or planning. Rags was fickle. Angel supposed it was just that he was so very young. Still, Angel could not remember that she had ever said things without thought, even when she was Rags's age.

"Floats have to have a sort of theme," said Rudy, with a crayon in his hand. "It is a Memorial Day parade, but I don't think every float has to be about soldiers or war."

"I think," said Angel slowly, "that our float should have entertainment as a theme."

Rudy and Mrs. O'Leary looked at Angel with approval. "Perfect!" said Rudy. "Our television station is mainly entertainment! And our show with clowns is definitely entertaining. At least I hope so," he added.

Rudy began to sketch a float while Mrs. O'Leary served lunch. After he sketched the float itself, Rudy stopped. "Now," he said, "what will be *on* the float? Besides just us," he added.

Angel's head was swimming with ideas. She had totally forgotten weddings (for the moment) and could hear the hoofbeats of the horses and the music of the marching bands. The mayor would be in an open car waving to the people crowding the curbs.

"I think," said Angel, "that something should be going on on the float. You know, we can't just stand there."

Rudy nodded.

"I think, right there on the float, clowns should be doing a show just like you do on TV."

Now Rudy was on his feet. "That's it!" he said. "A moving stage!"

"And on the side could be the words 'Let us entertain you!' " said Mrs. O'Leary.

Rudy sat down and drew a banner along the side of the float, and wrote the words on it. "Perfect!" he said. "We'll include our channel's name and number and it will be good advertising."

"We could even have children in the audience, on the float," said Angel.

"And they could participate," said Rudy, drawing in rows of folding chairs on the float. "Now, what kind of things should we do?"

"Magic," said Rags.

"That's good," said Rudy, who would never say anything Rags said was bad. "Everyone likes magic. We will have a magic show."

"And juggling," said Angel. "Kids like juggling."

Rudy nodded and began to make a list along the side of the picture. Rudy liked to make lists, too, Angel had noticed. He would fit into the family well. Mrs. O'Leary and Angel were always making lists.

"You can do the acts over again, because there

will be new people watching as the float moves along,'' said Mrs. O'Leary.

"That's a good idea," said Rudy, standing up. "I think we should go and price the lumber and crepe paper and decorations. And we have to find some wheels to mount it on."

"A hay wagon would be just right," said Mrs. O'Leary, remembering Margaret Toomer's brother in the country. "People borrow Margaret's brother's hay wagon for hayrides. I know he would let us use it, and the car could pull it."

While Rudy and Angel and Rags went to the lumber yard and to the store that sold crepe paper, Mrs. O'Leary called Margaret Toomer, who called her brother.

"He will be glad to lend you the wagon," said Margaret. "He rarely uses it anymore."

During the following weeks Angel and Rags and Edna helped Rudy build the float after school. They hammered and nailed and cut and pasted. Then they stopped for what Rudy called refresh-

ments. Refreshments meant supper at Smiley's, or a cone at Breezy Queen, or lemonade on the front porch. "We need refreshments because we work so hard," Rudy always said.

Gradually the float turned beautiful, and children were invited to be the audience (along with Angel and Rags and Edna). The acts were planned and practiced, and everything was ready for the big day. Rudy borrowed a garage to store the float in until Memorial Day.

It wasn't until the float was finished that Angel
had time to remember wedding plans. There
weren't any! She had been so busy with the float
that weeks had passed and still no photographer
was hired or invitations ordered or presents purchased. August would sneak up on them, thought
Angel, and it would be the wedding day and no
one would know what to do! She could picture
her mother, about to marry, with no wedding
dress, no cake, no presents, and no pictures. The

minister would say, "I'm sorry, I'm busy to-day," and go off to someone else's wedding. Her mother would stand at the altar in her flowered housedress, hair in a ponytail (the hairdresser would have been busy), and Rudy would snap his fingers and say, "Darn! Is it *today* we get married?"

No bakery would be able to bake a wedding cake so fast, so they would have to settle for one of the unsold, day-old cakes that Angel had seen on the bakery rack — the colored frosting slightly faded and run together, the roses flat and squashed, and the words HAPPY BIRTHDAY RICK or GET WELL PATTI written on the top instead of a freshly attired bride and groom. Angel shuddered as she thought of some of the leftover cakes she'd seen. She wondered why the cakes had never been used. Did the mothers of the birthday children and the sniffling sick girl forget? How careless of a mother. Or perhaps they were sample cakes. Angel felt better about that. She hated to think of careless, forgetful mothers.

But sample cakes or not, they would not do for

3.
The Temporarily Misplaced Town

But the next day something happened to make Angel forget wedding plans again.

"Angel," called Mrs. O'Leary, up the staircase, "Rudy and I are going to the city to shop today. Remember to keep your eye on Rags. We're taking the nine o'clock train, because the car needs some engine work and Rudy can't get it in until next week."

Angel turned over in bed. Was her mother finally going to shop for a wedding dress? Angel yawned. She had not babysat Rags for a long time. Usually Rudy insisted they take her or Rags or both of them along on these excursions.

"When will you be home?" called Angel.

her mother's wedding. And it looked as though her mother's wedding cake might have a baseball mitt on it, done in day-old chocolate, or a blue sailboat, unless she, Angel, took over and did some planning, fast. At the very least, it was her duty to inform her mother of how much work a wedding could be and warn her to start making plans.

"By dinner time," said her mother.

Angel's mother's voice trailed off as she left with Rudy. Angel got out of bed and began to wash and get dressed. Rags was already up, she noticed. She went downstairs and poured herself a bowl of cereal. The house was quiet and the only sound she heard was Rags crunching his Vitasnaps. Although school wasn't yet out for the summer, it was a free day because the teachers were having an end-of-the-year meeting. A fine, long day was ahead, but Angel had to babysit. She sighed and ate her cereal.

Rags seemed to be in a hurry. He finished breakfast quickly and slid down from his chair and put his bowl into the sink. He was just slipping out the back door, when Angel called, "Where are you going?"

"Nowhere."

"You can't go *nowhere*. You have to be *some*place."

Rags could see that Angel was not going to be satisfied unless she knew his whereabouts. "I'm not going far," he said.

Since Rags was about to enter kindergarten next year, Mrs. O'Leary had decided he should be allowed to go out of the yard by himself, so Angel could no longer say, "Stay in the yard."

"Don't get into any trouble," Angel said instead.

"I won't," he called, plainly in a hurry.

Angel propped the cereal box up in front of her dish so that she could study the gifts she could get by sending in boxtops of Vitasnap, and two dollars in cash. As she finished her second bowl of cereal, there was a knock at the back door.

Edna stood there, her bike leaning against the fence.

"Let's go on a bike ride," she said.

"I have to babysit," said Angel. "My mom has gone shopping in the city."

Edna thought about that for a minute. She frowned. "We can't waste a perfectly good day of vacation," she said.

Angel glanced at the back yard. Rags was kicking dirt in the driveway. He looked restless.

"We could take just a short bike ride," said Edna. "To the park, and back."

Angel looked at Rags again. "I suppose we could," she said. "After all, Rags is going to school in the fall. He has to be on his own then."

"Edna and I are going to ride our bikes for a little while," she called to Rags. "We'll be right back." Angel's mother always said, "We will be right back," when she went out. Angel thought of it as a warning, not as a lie. It gave the children confidence that she would not be gone long, as well as warned them not to be in trouble since she could show up unexpectedly at any moment.

"Will you be all right?" Angel asked.

Rags nodded. He hovered around the garage door.

The girls got onto their bikes, said "Giddap!" and were off down Kilbourn Avenue. It was a warm spring day, just right for a bike ride. Before long they had passed the park and gone to the edge of town, following a dirt road into the country.

"We should have brought a picnic," said Edna.

"If we come to a store, I can buy us candy bars," said Angel, who had some quarters from Rudy in her pocket.

The girls turned onto the roads that looked the prettiest — the ones that wound around trees and up hills. They came to a country store and purchased candy bars. They sat under an oak tree in a meadow and ate them. The warm sun on their hair made them sleepy.

"Let's race our horses!" said Edna suddenly.

The girls got up and brushed off and mounted their steeds. They raced down the road to mailboxes, barns, and crossroads. When they grew tired and stopped to rest, Angel said, "I think we'd better turn around and start home."

The girls got back on their bikes and pedaled along the road. After a while, Edna said, "I didn't see that round barn before, did you?"

Angel had to admit that she did not recognize it.

"We didn't come this way," said Edna. "All these roads look alike. They don't even have signs."

The girls stood with their bikes at a crossroads that could be any of the many crossroads they had passed.

"Which way do you think we should go?" said Angel, feeling nervous.

"Eenie meenie miny moe," said Edna, pointing.

"That is no way to decide how to get home," said Angel crossly. Edna could afford to guess at roads. She didn't have a small brother at home she was supposed to be tending.

"I think it's this road," said Edna, pointing. "I remember that windmill."

Angel looked doubtful, but the girls started down the road she had chosen.

After they had been riding for a long time, there seemed to be more country and trees and fewer farms and no town.

"I think we're going away from town," said

Angel, stopping her bike in a cloud of dust. Both girls felt warm and dusty now, and thirsty for a cold drink.

"We could find the direction by the sun," said Edna, who was usually very knowledgeable and dependable in a crisis. "When the sun does down, that is the west. But it's right overhead now, so we can't tell what direction it is."

"We can't wait till the sun goes down!" said Angel, stamping her foot. "My mom will be home by then, and Rags needs his lunch! And even if we knew where west is, how would that help us? If we don't know where we are, how can we tell which direction to go?"

The girls followed two more small roads, but ended up back at the same crossroads they'd left from.

"I think we are lost," said Angel softly, feeling tears behind her eyelids.

"We can't be lost," Edna scoffed. "We just are temporarily turned around."

Even though Edna's words were no solution, they reassured Angel. Edna was right; they had just temporarily misplaced their town. It had to be somewhere nearby.

By the time the girls came to a farmhouse, the sun was no longer overhead, but definitely west.

"I'll ask the farm people how to get to town," said Edna. Edna always showed more confidence than Angel in these situations.

The girls rode up the dusty, rutted driveway, past tall fields of something green, and knocked on the door. A woman in an apron came to the door.

"Pardon me," said Edna politely, "but could you tell us the way to town?"

The woman invited the girls in and asked them what town they were looking for. That made Angel wonder how far they had come! Were they near another town, instead of their own?

"Elm City," said Edna. "Wisconsin," she added, just in case they had really gone far and were in another state, like Minnesota or Iowa.

"You've come a long way," said the woman, pouring some cold milk for the girls and putting a plate of warm cookies in front of them.

Then she drew a map on the back of an old envelope, moistening the pencil point in her mouth several times to be sure it wrote dark enough for the girls to follow. When they left, she pointed up the road, saying, "Don't forget, left at the round barn, right at the bridge, and right again at the railroad crossing."

The girls thanked her over and over again, as they set out, refreshed, in the right direction.

"This is the road I thought we should take," said Edna.

It was safe to say that now, thought Angel, when they knew the way.

The closer they got to town, the more nervous Angel felt. What if her mother and Rudy had returned and Rags was missing? What if Rags was starving, or had run away looking for Angel, or had found matches to play with and set the house afire? Even if he was all right, her mother would not be pleased to find him alone. Angel pedaled faster as they drew nearer to town.

"Slow down," called Edna, who was tired from pumping up the hills.

"I can't," said Angel. "I have to get home."

The last few blocks down Kilbourn Avenue seemed to take forever. Finally Angel could see their green house on the corner. When she arrived she ran up the back steps and into the house. It was as quiet as when she'd left it, the clock ticking and refrigerator gently purring. No sign of her mother or Rudy. Angel felt happy to see they weren't home yet. But then she noticed there was no sign of Rags either. She ran outside and looked under the porch. His city was quiet and unattended.

"Rags?" she called. "Rags, where are you?"

After a minute or two, the garage door opened. Rags looked different somehow, but Angel was so glad to see him, she didn't care how he looked. She ran to him and threw her arms around him and gave him a big hug.

"Are you all right?" she said. "We got lost, and it got late . . ." Angel went on explaining to Rags and apologizing, but Rags didn't seem to care.

"Of course I'm all right," he said.

It was not until then that Angel noticed what was different about Rags. He was red. Not just his cheeks and lips, which were meant to be red, or at least pink, but his ears and his hair and his hands as well. Even his clothes were red.

"What's that?" said Angel. "What *is* that red stuff all over you?"

But then Angel knew. She could smell it.

"Paint!" she said.

"Paint," repeated Rags, answering her question.

By now Edna had ridden up to the gate and tied her horse to the fence. She fell onto the back steps, exhausted, and pointed at Rags.

"What happened to Rags?" she said.

Angel repeated her question. "What did you do?" she demanded. "Why are you covered with paint?"

Angel was already thinking of how to get it off of Rags before her mother got home. What could she use? Turpentine? Paint remover? She would have to throw his clothes away. Still, it could have been worse. Rags was safe. No other damage was done. There were worse things in the world than paint. But there was no time to lose. She had to get Rags into the bathtub. Or basement. She led him into the house and got some newspapers and a stiff brush. She would have to work fast.

Edna joined in, rubbing at Rags's hair with a washcloth. "This stuff doesn't come out," she said. "We might have to take him to one of those places where they dip furniture to remove the paint. My mom had some chairs dipped and all the paint came off, whiz bang, like magic."

Angel hoped fervently that they did not have to dip Rags.

As they rubbed, Edna said, "Why were you playing in the paint?"

"Wasn't," muttered Rags. "I wasn't playing."

"What were you doing, then?" said Angel, not really caring if she could just clean him up before her mother saw him.

"I made a wedding present," said Rags proudly.

"You should use your water colors to paint a picture, Rags. Not this stuff that you paint a house with."

Rags was shaking his head. "Not a picture," he was saying. "Not a house. I painted Rudy's *car*! For a wedding present. He wanted a new car."

Angel sat down on the nearest chair. She was wrong. Cleaning up Rags was not solving the problem. There was a bigger problem, she knew now. And it was outside, in the garage.

4.
Trouble in the Garage

"You *what?*" shouted Edna to Rags.

"I painted the car," he repeated. "For a wedding present."

Angel and Edna forgot about getting any more paint off of Rags. There was something much more important to think about before Rudy and Angel's mother returned. The two girls ran down the steps and out the door and into the garage. There on the workbench was an open can of paint. Beside it was a brush. And all over the workbench, and the floor, and even the wall, was paint. Drops and splashes and smears and even little puddles. But worst of all, was Rudy's car. Once blue, it now had streaks of a sort of electric red running around it.

The girls stood beside it and stared. No one seemed to know what to say. Even Edna couldn't say anything more than, "Wow!" Finally, Angel found she could move, and she walked slowly around the car, hoping that the back and other side would be paint-free. They weren't. Only the very top was still blue.

"I couldn't reach the top," said Rags, feeling he needed to apologize for the incomplete job. "I'll stand on a chair and finish it later."

Angel ran her finger over a red streak, hoping that it was still wet and that they could wipe it off with a rag. But no, Rags had used fast-drying latex paint, guaranteed to cover in one coat, and dry in an hour, or your money back.

"Some places show through," said Rags. "It needs another coat, but I got tired." Here Rags sat down on a box and sighed. The girls did not seem to be very complimentary, and he had worked so hard all afternoon. He had expected more praise from them. Well, the important thing was that Rudy and his mother would like it. After all, it was their wedding present. Not Angel's.

Angel opened the garage door to let fresh air in. The paint smell was beginning to make her stomach ache. Or maybe it was fear that was making her sick. She stood, thinking of all the things she wanted to say to Rags, to *do* to Rags. She thought about lashing out at him, asking him questions like "Why did you do this?" or "How could you do such a dumb, dumb thing?" She wanted to pick Rags up by his ears and shake him till he rattled (something that Angel had heard a mean teacher say once). She wanted to leave home, be an only child, or at least keep her mother and Rudy out of the garage.

"We should *never* have gone on a bike ride," Angel said at last. "I was supposed to babysit. If I had been here, none of this would have happened."

Rags had a surprised look on his face. "You don't like it!" he said. Sensing disapproval, he began to cry.

"Oh, stop it, Rags," said Angel, "or I'll give you something to cry about."

Angel would have said much more — things

like Rags was old enough to know better — except for the fact that she felt it was partially her fault. She felt guilty for leaving Rags in the first place.

"How about paint remover?" said Edna. She did not feel she could comfort Angel, or scold Rags either, because part of her felt it was her fault too. She should not have urged Angel to leave Rags.

"Don't take the paint *off*!" cried Rags. "I had to work hard to get it so — pretty."

"It is *not* pretty, Rags. Don't you know pretty when you see it? It's ugly and awful, and what will Rudy say?"

"Maybe he'll sue you," said Edna softly.

Could that be true, wondered Angel. Could one's very own almost-family sue? Would the whole family have to appear in court with little Rags, paint-smeared, unable to sign his name in cursive writing, standing too low for the judge to see? Did they have lawyers to defend children? Would Rags be jailed at so tender an age, or sent to nursery reform school?

"Rudy will *like* it," said Rags. "He will say, 'Thank you for the wonderful wedding present, Rags. It was just what I wanted.' He told me that he wanted the car painted. He told us, Angel, don't you remember?"

Angel did remember. Rudy did speak about getting the car painted before the wedding. But it had never occurred to Angel that Rags would get it into his mind to do it! Where in the world did Rags get such wild ideas? Where did he ever get such an imagination? Their mother should talk to Rags before his imagination got him into real trouble.

"I think we should try paint remover," repeated Edna.

Despite Rags's pleas that it was pretty and Rudy wanted his car painted, Angel and Edna searched the garage and basement for paint remover. All they could find was an old can of turpentine. While Rags cried, the girls dabbed old rags in the potent liquid and rubbed away at the red streaks. It was ten minutes of hard work before any of their effort showed, and then only a tiny bit of the red paint came off.

"My rag is *blue*!" said Edna. "I think more of the blue paint is coming off than the red."

"We don't want that," said Angel in alarm. "Don't take the blue off, Edna! Then we'll have more trouble than ever."

Angel noticed her rag was blue too, and the two girls sat down to think about what the next step should be.

"It needs to be dipped," said Edna. "Like my mother's chairs. Instead of dipping Rags, we should dip the car."

The sun that had been almost in the west when the girls were on their bike ride was now definitely setting. Angel knew her mother and Rudy would walk in any moment, and she couldn't think of a single thing to do about it. It looked (as Alyce often said) as if she would have to take her lumps.

"I s'pose I should go home," said Edna. "My mom will be calling because it's getting dark."

Lucky Edna. She could leave, free as a bird. No little brother to get her into trouble. No lumps waiting at home for her. Just a nice dinner with normal family conversation about the day's activities. She probably wouldn't even mention Rags's trouble. "We went on a nice bike ride out in the country," she'd probably say.

Her mother would say, "How nice, dear. I hope you were careful and watched for cars at the intersections." Edna would say yes, of course she did, and calmly eat her dessert, all thoughts of Rags and Angel's lumps forgotten.

Edna waved to Angel as she started home. "See you tomorrow," she called.

Angel watched her ride down the street. Then she and Rags sat on the back steps. Angel could not remember when she had felt so discouraged. She hated to disappoint her mother, who was so good to her, and Rudy, who trusted her and whom she loved. He would probably say, "I guess I didn't know Angel as well as I thought I did. I thought she was dependable."

Tears welled up in Angel's eyes at the thought

of disappointing her new father-to-be. Perhaps he would say, "The wedding is off. I don't want to marry anyone who has a daughter I can't trust."

Angel saw her mother, her head in her hands, pleading with Rudy for another chance, even wishing she didn't have children at all, perhaps. Maybe Angel and Rags should go to an orphanage and save her mother's marriage. Where *was* an orphanage? she wondered. The only one she remembered was in the movie *Annie*. There surely wasn't one around Elm City.

By the time Rudy and her mother came up the walk, Angel was crying so hard that she didn't hear them. Rags, seeing Angel cry, felt things must be very bad indeed, and cried harder than ever himself.

Seeing them, their mother and Rudy ran up the steps and swept them into their arms.

"What is it?" cried their mother. "What is the matter, Angel?"

Realizing that they were home and that the terrible truth had to be faced head-on made Angel cry even harder.

"Rudy, they must be *ill!*" said their mother. "Perhaps they have food poisoning or appendicitis!"

Rudy picked Rags up and felt his bones. "Nothing's broken!" he said cheerfully. "What about you, Angel? Are you all in one piece?"

"Something awful has happened," said Angel's mother, on the verge of tears now herself.

"It couldn't be too bad," said Rudy cheerfully, "or they couldn't make this much noise. They don't seem ill, and the house is still standing," he said, looking in the back door.

"It's worse than that," sobbed Angel.

"Nothing is worse than you or Rags being sick or injured," said Rudy. "And you both seem fine, so I'm not worried," he said, going into the house with the bags and boxes from the day's shopping trip.

Angel felt a little better by Rudy's calm attitude. But when she told him, and when he saw his very own car with red stripes on it, his attitude would change, Angel thought soberly.

"So what did you do today, you two rascals?"

said Rudy, sitting on the step beside them.

Angel burst into tears again. Rags climbed up on Rudy's lap. He pulled at Rudy's tie, as he said in a small voice, "I made you a wedding present."

"Ho *ho!*" said Rudy. "That surely doesn't sound bad, does it?" he said, looking at Angel's mother.

Angel's mother looked skeptical.

"It's a surprise," said Rags, sniffling. "It's in the garage."

Well, the cat was out of the bag now, thought Angel.

"Let's all go see it!" said Rudy, standing up and putting his arm around Rags's small shoulders.

As Rudy opened the garage door and turned on the light, Angel cried, "It's all my fault. Edna and I went for a bike ride and got lost and when we got home Rags was — all finished."

In the brightly lit garage, the painted car seemed to stand in a spotlight. The red streaks seemed even more vibrant, Angel thought.

"Isn't it pretty?" cried Rags. "Do you like it, do you like it?"

Mrs. O'Leary stood with a puzzled look on her face. But very quickly the puzzled look changed to an impatient look, and then to a very, very cross one.

"Rags did this?" she said. "Rags did *this*? He did it himself?"

"I did it all alone," said Rags proudly. "Angel wasn't even here."

Now the cross look shifted to Angel. Her mother opened her mouth to say something (like, "I thought I could trust you, Angel"), but no words came out. She looked back at Rags as if she was going to say something to him (like, "You are old enough to know better, Rags"), but now Rudy had put his hand up, like a stop sign, Angel thought. On his face, Angel seemed to detect a smile. Surely he could not be smiling!

Rags had a very tight hold of Rudy's other hand. "Do you like it?" he whispered. "It is my wedding present to you. You said you wanted the car painted."

"Yes," said Rudy clearly. "I did say I wanted the car painted. How did you know that red was my favorite color, Rags?"

By now Angel's mother was very red in the face. She looked as if she might explode. But Rudy put his arm around her, and said, "This is our very first wedding present. And it is probably the most — ah — thoughtful."

He gave her a squeeze. Then they both burst out laughing. Angel's mother laughed and laughed until the red in her face was gone and she didn't look as though she was about to explode anymore. Now Angel felt cross. Couldn't parents even be counted on to be angry when they should? Did Rudy and her mom know the seriousness of this? She had disobeyed them, and Rags should have known better. And all they could do was stand there and laugh. If Angel had known this, she would not have had to spend most of the afternoon in panic and tears. The more they laughed, the angrier she felt. She would have welcomed a good lecture on obedience and dependability.

"See," said Rags, on the way into the house, "I told you Rudy would like it! He *does* think it's pretty! Angel said it was ugly," he said, turning to his mother.

"I think we have to have a serious talk," said Angel's mother.

"Tomorrow," said Rudy. "Our burgers will be ice cold if we don't eat them right now." He reached for a large bag with SMILEY's written on it and distributed hamburgers and French fries and milk shakes to everyone. Angel had not known how hungry she was, until she began to eat. And as she ate, her anger faded and her good spirits returned. Rudy had smoothed over the crisis again and made things feel better. He was right — the best time for a serious talk was tomorrow. By that time everyone would be rested and not hungry, and they would be able to see the red and blue car in a whole new light!

5.
Rain Before Seven

The next morning Rudy took Angel and her mother aside and said that although Rags must be warned against painting objects at random, there was no harm done. After all, the car had needed to be painted anyway, and now they would get their money's worth. Meanwhile, they could enjoy Rags's creativity and good will. Rudy did not want to repaint the car too soon and make Rags feel as if his gift was not thoughtful.

"It's silly to be upset by small things," said Rudy.

That sounded like good advice to Angel. But how was she to know what was small and what was big? To most people, red streaks on their car would not be small.

After Rudy gave Rags a sensible talk in the dining room, Mrs. O'Leary gave him another sensible talk in his room. (She did not share Rudy's view on what was big and what was small.) Rags was confined to his room for a few hours to think about what he had done, and Angel to hers to remember that when she was babysitting, it meant she should be in the same house as the "baby."

Rudy drove the blue car with the red stripes back and forth to work and all around town, and when people asked about it, he said proudly, "It's a wedding present." He even (against better judgment, Angel and her mother thought) decided to drive it in the parade. It would pull the float proudly down Main Street in all of its blue and red glory! Rudy did not appear in any hurry at all to take it to "Car Renew" for its real paint job. Angel fervently hoped that it would be painted in time for the wedding. A bride and groom certainly could not ride in a striped car. Weddings were serious business, and the car was very undignified.

* * *

Memorial Day and its parade came closer every day. The float was ready and waiting, and Rudy started practicing with the children the acts that they would put on, on the "moving stage." He had given Rags the responsibility for the trained-dog show. The dogs were already trained, so all Rags had to do was learn their names and commands by heart and put them through their acts. Rags learned very quickly and soon the dogs were performing perfectly. Angel and Edna had all of the "audience" selected and folding chairs set up for them. She and Edna were in Rudy's "band," which played funny instruments like combs and pots and pans and whistles and toy drums. During rehearsal the "combs" acted silly quite often, combing one another's hair between acts, and Rudy had to say, "That's enough, boys!" in a very gruff sort of voice. The gruff voice surprised everyone, especially Angel. It was the closest Rudy ever came to being angry, thought Angel.

The act before theirs was a horse act, and it was fun to watch the horses toss their manes and paw the air and eat sugar lumps while their masters brushed and curried them.

Behind Rudy's float was a department store float with slim girls modeling the latest fashions. Angel and Edna thought it would be fun to be a model. Secretly they wished they were on that float instead of the dog act float.

Memorial Day dawned bright and sunny, but by the time the O'Learys sat down for breakfast, the sky had clouded over. Mrs. O'Leary looked out the kitchen window and frowned. A few random drops of water had appeared on the pane.

"Is that thunder?" said Angel, from the breakfast table.

"I think it is," said her mother.

"What will we do if it rains?" said Angel. She thought of the floats with their crepe-paper decorations. She thought of the people along the curb, getting wet. Maybe the people would even stay home altogether if it rained. The only audience they would have could be the small one riding on the float.

"Perhaps Rudy should have had a top on the float," she said with a worried look on her face.

"A roof! A roof! That's what we need," cried Rags.

"It's too late for that," said their mother, sighing.

By the time Rudy arrived at the back door in the blue and red car it was raining in earnest. But despite the rain, Rudy had a big smile on his face. He did not even seem to notice it was raining!

"Happy Memorial Day!" he shouted, scooping Rags up onto his shoulders. Rags was squealing and laughing and saying to Rudy, "We need a roof! We need a roof!"

"On the float," said Angel, explaining that the rain would ruin the parade. Why in the world hadn't Rudy thought of that? And prepared for it?

"A little rain never hurt anything," said Rudy. "We can run between the drops."

"Can the float run between the drops, too?" said Rags, acting silly now. Rags often acted silly around Rudy, Angel thought, because Rudy never minded silliness as her mother did.

"Actually," said Rudy, "the parade is not until two o'clock. It will stop raining by that time. It is going to rain all morning and make everything clean and fresh and green for us, and then it will stop just in time for the parade! You wait and see!"

Rags went with Rudy to put last-minute touches on the float and get the dogs and their cages in place while the float was still in the dry garage. Then Rudy had to get into his clown costume and dress Rags in his dog-show clothes and organize the other participants, who were assembling at one o'clock. Angel and her mother waited at home, watching the sky for a sign of the sun.

"Those raindrops on the window this morning were a bad omen," said Mrs. O'Leary. "I feel a bit uneasy about the parade."

"It's going to clear up by noon," said Angel, bravely, not really believing what she said.

Her mother shook her head. "I don't think so," she said. "Rain before seven, clear before eleven; but the rain started after seven. It looks like an all-day storm."

Thunder followed her menacing words, and a bolt of lightning lit up the dark living room. "It's not a good sign," she said.

Usually it was Angel who took the dark, worried view of things. Now that her mother was so glum, Angel felt called upon to cheer her up.

"That's just superstition," she said. "Nothing will go wrong. A little rain never hurt anyone."

She repeated Rudy's words, but she did not have Rudy's faith in them, or his hearty smile.

At noon, it was still raining. Mrs. O'Leary silently got out plastic raincoats and umbrellas and rubber boots and put them by the door. At one o'clock Rudy and Rags drove up in the blue and red car to collect them. The rain was coming down in torrents. The red brush marks on the car shone like the sun. The rain did not touch those, thought Angel. The things the rain should fade remained as bright as ever. But what would happen to the colored crepe paper on the float?

Rudy was humming a parade song as he bundled them into the car, but everyone else was very quiet. The humming and the rain on the car roof were the only sounds all the way to the garage where the float was kept.

On the float (still safe and dry) were the audience in their folding chairs, the dogs with wagging tails, and the rest of the people in the show. Rudy turned on the portable tape player that was to be music for the show, and directed it into a loudspeaker on the float. Parade music poured out, loud and gay.

"We tried to put a tarp up over the stage and the audience," Rudy explained, "but when we opened the garage door the strong wind blew it down. It's no good in this wind."

"The roof went poof! The roof went poof!" sang Rags loudly.

"That's right." Rudy laughed. "That is exactly what it did."

Rudy encouraged Rags with his silly rhymes, thought Angel.

Rudy looked at his watch. "Well, I guess we can't wait any longer," he said. "Put your umbrellas up!"

He began to back the float out of the garage and drive to the corner of Main Street and Highway Nine, where the parade was to begin.

"Why don't they postpone the parade?" asked Angel, to anyone who was listening.

"How can they?" said Edna. "There is only one Memorial Day a year. You can't celebrate a holiday like this in June or July. It's not the same."

But as the red crepe paper ran into the green, and the blue circles on Rudy's and Rags's faces ran into the orange ones, Edna had some second thoughts about the holiday herself. A sunny June Memorial Day might be preferable to this soaking wet May one.

As the parade began, Rudy's float took its place in line behind the prancing wet horses and high school band. Angel noticed that some of the floats did have roofs that stayed on, but for the most part their decorations (including the department store models) were as wet as their own. Rags was throwing wet candy to the cheering crowd, and Rudy was waving and smiling just as if he were not soaking wet. In their act, the rain had given Rudy and Rags and other actors an opportunity to use umbrellas to do funny things with. One of the clowns held his umbrella upside down and, when it was filled with water, turned it over his head.

"Not many people stayed home!" shouted Edna, waving a wet hand to the audience.

Rudy and the clowns finished their act, to loud applause. Now it was time for the dog show. When the float stopped (the whole parade seemed to stop every five minutes), Rudy said, "Let's get the dogs out and onto their chairs, Rags!"

Rags opened the cages and led each dog to the chair he was used to. They sat quietly, just as they had in the rehearsal, waiting for Rags to give orders. When the last dog was on his chair, and Rags was just about to give orders, the parade moved forward again, and Rudy's float started with a terrible jerk. The sudden movement frightened the dogs on the chairs, and one

after the other they sprang down to the floor and
out into the audience!

Mrs. O'Leary, who had predicted disaster, was
now laughing (or maybe it was just a grin-and-
bear-it smile, thought Angel). At any rate, Angel
was pleased she was no longer pouting and was
taking it less seriously.

Angel and Edna and some other children in the
audience, as well as Rags and Rudy, ran after the
dogs, crawling under chairs and over decorations.

The dogs, frightened even more at being chased by strangers, jumped off the float and onto Main Street and ran into the crowds of cheering people.

"Get that dog!" shouted Rags, jumping over the side of the float after a small black poodle. Angel and Edna ran after two terriers but lost them in the crowd.

The parade stopped again, having gone only a short distance, and people along the street began to help with the chase.

"Here, Crosby," shouted Rags to the black poodle. "Come on, fellow, come on back!"

Crosby, who had no intention of coming back, was huddled under a parked car. The parade started up again, and was half over by the time all of the dogs were finally rounded up and carried back to their cages on the float.

By that time Rudy decided they had better forget about the dog show to prevent the whole thing from happening again. The police had had to help gather the dogs, and Rudy was sure they would not look favorably on being called on again to crawl under cars and search behind buildings.

By the end of the parade, everyone was soaked to the skin, but they were laughing. With the rain still coming down, Rudy parked the float back in the garage, unhitched it from the car, and took all of the wet participants in his float to Smiley's for hamburgers. It was warm and dry in Smiley's, and everyone piled into the plastic booths with their raincoats and wet jeans sloshing up and down. Now that it was all over, it seemed even funnier than it had at the time.

Mrs. O'Leary and Rudy and Alyce and Margaret and Margaret's brother and Edna and Angel and Rags all went back to the O'Learys' house to dry out and drink hot cocoa and sit in front of the artificial fireplace.

The children re-enacted the dog chase until no one could stop laughing.

Mrs. O'Leary kept repeating, "I knew something awful would happen when I saw that rain on the window this morning . . ."

And Rudy (his arms around Angel and Rags) said, "I'll bet this is a Memorial Day we won't forget!"

"It's always darkest before the dawn," said Alyce, mysteriously.

Angel didn't know what that had to do with anything, but everyone else nodded and agreed. It was definitely a holiday they would all remember, whether it was darkest before the dawn or not!

6.
Single Living?

The day after Memorial Day was bright and sunny, without a cloud in the sky. Even the grass and trees and flowers and ground were dry.

"This is the day that should have been Memorial Day," grumbled Angel to Edna on the way to school.

The girls were going to school to get their report cards and books and papers and pencils and take them home. They were also going to clean out desks and help the janitor close up the school for the summer. The school year was over at last and the long-awaited vacation had arrived.

By noon, classes were dismissed, and loud whooping cries filled the air. Some of the students didn't even take their books and papers home, but threw them into the rubbish bin on the playground.

"Now it's really summer," said Angel. "Nothing to do but ride our bikes and go swimming at the pool."

"What about the wedding?" demanded Edna. "Are the invitations ordered? And the flowers and stuff? You will need the whole summer to get ready for the wedding!"

Angel had almost forgotten about the wedding! It was strange how something so important could be forgotten, even temporarily. There seemed to be something going on every minute to distract her from the big event in August, like getting lost, the painted car, and the rainy Memorial Day parade.

"My mom and Rudy haven't even mentioned it," said Angel.

"Maybe it's off," said Edna, mysteriously. "Maybe they are not getting married after all."

Angel looked doubtful. She would have heard if that had happened. Her mother would be upset.

Rudy would be upset. He would probably even leave town.

"I don't think so," said Angel.

"My mom's friend Molly called her wedding off at the last minute," said Edna cheerfully. "Everything was planned, too. She just changed her mind at the last minute."

Angel frowned. Would her mother do that? Was she keeping it a secret that she had changed her mind? It was surely true that the wedding was never mentioned.

"We had these new dresses," Edna went on. "You know, mother-daughter dresses, for Molly's wedding. But it was okay, they weren't too fancy, we could wear them other places."

It would be awful if something happened at the last minute, thought Angel, even if they could wear their dresses later.

"Better now than later," said Edna wisely, as if she were reading Angel's mind. "Some people go through with the wedding just because it's planned. That's why there are so many divorces."

Angel could not figure out how Edna knew so much. Angel did not know a single thing about divorce, even though her mother must have gotten one. Was that what had happened with Angel's father? Had her mother gone through with the wedding and found out later that it was a mistake? Well, she must have! And now perhaps she was not willing to risk making the same mistake twice! Better now than later! Her mother was not talking about the wedding because there *was* no wedding! She had changed her mind!

"Let's ride our horses," Edna was saying.

How could Angel think of horses (or bikes) when her mother's wedding was probably off? Well, maybe it was good the invitations weren't ordered. They could even have been sent, and that would be very embarrassing. What if wedding presents had begun to come in and the cake ordered and even (heaven forbid) the day itself should arrive and the organ music have to be halted in the middle of "Here Comes the Bride"! No, Angel could not go on a bike ride this afternoon. She had to know the worst. She did not want to be in the dark any longer.

When Angel turned in at her gate, Edna followed her. No one was home. Rags must be with Mom or Rudy, thought Angel.

She set her books on the dining room table and looked around the room for signs of a canceled wedding. Everything was just as it had been. Rags's Matchbox cars were underfoot, his coloring book open on the table. A dress pattern of Alyce's was on the chair. The faucet dripped noisily in the sink.

Angel wandered into the living room, where one of her mother's magazines lay open on the sofa. Edna pointed. "Look!" she said. "*Single Living*." Edna rolled her eyes. Angel had never seen that magazine in the house before . . . Was it a newly acquired subscription to help her mother get through a canceled wedding? Angel felt it was an omen. It meant something. People did not read *Single Living* if they were planning a wedding! They read things like *The Bride* or *Family Circle* or *Good Housekeeping*!

"Why would your mom read *that*, if she was getting married?" Edna asked. Angel did not need to be reminded.

She paged through the magazine. The table of contents listed articles called "Cooking for One" and "How to Start Dating Again," "Living Without a Mate" and "Do Your Children Really Need a Father?"

"You're right," said Angel. More and more the magazine seemed to be an omen.

Angel began to look around the house with Edna's eyes. It took on the appearance of the home of a single woman.

"There should be *lists*," said Edna, sitting on the edge of an armchair and swinging a foot. "No one gets married without making lots and lots of lists. Do you see any lists around?"

The girls ran to the desk and to the counter. Even in Mrs. O'Leary's bedroom they did not find a list. Finally, on the table near her mother's reading glasses, Angel found a bit of paper.

"It's a list!" she shouted to Edna, as if it made everything all right again.

Edna picked it up. "It's a grocery list," she said. " 'Canned peas, bread, milk, bananas,' " she read.

Angel's face fell.

"Nope," said Edna. "She's not getting married. That's all there is to it." Edna's voice sounded final.

By the time Mrs. O'Leary came home from work and Rags came in with Rudy, Edna had gone home, and Angel was convinced that the wedding was off. She was already missing Rudy, feeling him gone, his room empty, his red and blue car headed for Washington. Was it something she had done?

The sooner she knew, the better. No sense in delaying bad news. Rudy was carrying in bags of groceries, and her mother was putting them into the cupboard and refrigerator.

"Why aren't you getting married?" Angel burst out when she got to the kitchen.

Her mother stopped what she was doing and

stood with a can of garden peas in her hand.

"Because it is not August," she said.

"You mean you *are* getting married in August?" Angel asked.

"Of course," said her mother. "Angel, you knew that. You knew that a long time ago!"

"I thought you changed your mind," said Angel, who by now had done such a good job of convincing herself that she was not even sure whether to believe her mother or not.

"Well, you would surely know it if we changed our minds!" said her mother, setting the peas on the shelf by a can of young carrots.

"Edna's mother's friend changed her mind," said Angel. "Edna said 'Better now than later,' and that magazine in the living room is for single people."

"That is Alyce's magazine," said Mrs. O'Leary. "She brought it over to show me a recipe for Sour Cherry Soup."

"There!" said Rudy, setting the last bag of groceries on the counter. "That's it for the stockpile!"

Angel hoped her mother would not tell Rudy that she thought the wedding was off. She did not want to be embarrassed all over again.

Rudy said he was making his famous spaghetti dinner with garlic bread that evening, so Angel and Rags and their mother were shooed into the living room until it was ready. Angel thought it was the perfect time (why put it off any longer?) to warn her mother that *if* she *was* going to marry, weddings were a lot of work and needed much planning in advance. Surely it could not wait any longer. It was already June.

"School is out for good," said Angel, giving her mother a sense of what time of year it was. She hoped her mother would not remember report cards right now when she wanted to talk about the wedding.

"The whole summer is ahead of you now!" said her mother.

"Well . . . it will go fast," replied Angel. "It's barely three months long. Not even twelve weeks. Less than ninety days . . ." Angel was very good in arithmetic. She always got an *A*.

"Oh, summer is long when you are young," said her mother.

That seemed a silly thing to say. It was the same length whether you were ten or eighty, after all.

Her mother began reminiscing about her own childhood now, getting completely off the subject.

"I hear printers are really busy in the summer," said Angel casually.

"Printers?" said her mother, as if she had never heard the word before.

Angel sighed. Her mother was not making this easy. "The people who print wedding invitations," said Angel clearly. She cleared her throat. "Have you ordered any yet?" she said in what she hoped was a casual voice.

Rudy's voice came from the kitchen, asking where the crushed red pepper was. Angel's mother excused herself and went to find it. When she returned, as Angel feared, she had forgotten the question and the subject of the conversation altogether.

"I love spaghetti," said her mother, leaning back on the sofa. "We all like it, even Rags."

Angel agreed that they all loved spaghetti.

"Especially Rudy's spaghetti," her mother added. "It's got some just-right spice in it!"

It certainly did not seem to Angel that her mother was in the least anxious to get married. Or even talk about weddings. You would think that she got married every day, she treated it so casually.

Now she was going on about someone at work who had lost ten pounds on a citrus diet. "Imagine, Angel, all she ate for three days was grapefruit."

Grapefruit did not seem as important as a wedding. Why did her mother care about diets?

"Bakers are really busy, too," said Angel. "With birthday cakes and wedding cakes and things . . ."

Her mother looked puzzled. "You both just

had your birthdays. And besides, I like to bake birthday cakes myself, Angel. You know how Rags loves that marble cake I make.''

Now Rags heard his name and climbed up on his mother's lap. ''Cake!'' he said. ''Make a cake! A cake to make! Candles to blow! Candles to grow!''

Mrs. O'Leary was patting Rags on the back now, and hugging him and ruffling his hair. Their thoughts were on birthdays. Angel had used the wrong clues.

''All the tulips are up in Margaret Toomer's garden,'' said Mrs. O'Leary suddenly. ''And our ferns are sprouting on the north side, do you know that, Angel? It will be time to plant the petunias any day now.''

''Florists are busy in summer,'' said Angel.

''I wouldn't think so,'' said her mother. ''People have flowers of their own in gardens in summer. They don't need florists the way they do in the winter. Or around Prom time.''

''They need them for weddings,'' said Angel

clearly. "They take orders for wedding bouquets
and things like that way ahead of time. Edna said
they are really busy in summer."

"Edna seems to know a lot about weddings,"
said Mrs. O'Leary, laughing.

"She does!" said Angel.

"Who wants to set the table?" called Rudy.
"Any little helpers in there?"

"He means you, Angel," said her mother. "I
am going to rest my eyes till dinner is ready."

Angel set the table and wondered how she was
ever going to convince her mother of her responsibility about this wedding. Now that she was
sure it was "on," it was absolutely necessary to
begin planning immediately. By the time Rudy
called them to the table, Angel was aching to
hear some plans being made.

"Pass the Parmesan, please, Angel," said her
mother.

"What day is the wedding?" burst out Angel.
"When are you going to order invitations? When
are we going to get dresses? And a cake, and

flowers? And you have no *lists* made!'' Angel's face turned red.

''Why, Angel! We have plenty of time to do all that,'' said her mother. ''Any day the end of August is all right, isn't it, Rudy? It could even be September . . .''

''We have to *know*,'' said Angel, feeling tears in her eyes now. Tears made her angry. And that made more tears come. ''You can't just buy invitations the day before! And get a minister and ring and flowers!''

''Is that true?'' said Rudy, winding the long spaghetti around his fork, and turning to Angel's mother to answer.

''Angel, this is going to be a small wedding. We are not going to have invitations and we will use flowers from the garden, and Margaret Toomer is going to make the wedding cake. I might even wear my blue silk dress that I got for the trip, and we can always find you a nice dress in time.''

So her mother *had* thought about the wedding.

Not a lot, but she had plans (of a sort) for a cake, and flowers, and a dress. But no invitations? What was a wedding without guests?

"We will just ask friends, we thought, Angel," said Rudy. "My parents will come, of course, and Alyce and Margaret and the people we love, but it will be a small wedding and we won't need printed invitations."

"After the wedding we will have some announcements printed, and send them out," her mother went on.

So her mother *had* planned on going to the printers. And getting announcements. She wondered if Edna ever heard of *that*.

Her mother reached across the table for Angel's hand. "I'm sorry you were worried, Angel," she said. "It is just that second weddings are not as — big or fancy — as first weddings."

"I don't know about that!" said Rudy, smiling. "This is my first wedding, and Angel and Rags's first wedding! It seems as if it should be very important!"

"It *is* important," said Angel's mother. "Important but not showy."

Rudy agreed he did not like showy. "It's mostly for us," he said. "The four of us."

"The main thing is that we will do everything in plenty of time," said Mrs. O'Leary. "And you are not to worry about a thing."

Angel felt a surge of relief in the pit of her stomach because she did not have to do all the planning herself. It would not be easy not to worry, but she would try. And the first thing she should do, she thought, was to stop listening to Edna! Edna not only knew a lot, she knew a little *too* much about a lot of things!

7.
A New Name for Angel

Vacation was now in full swing. The days spread out each morning full of promise for Angel and Edna. They rode their bikes (and did not get lost), and went to the park, and watched the men clean the swimming pool and get it ready to fill with water. The afternoon sun beat down on them and made their arms freckle and bleached their hair. As Alyce said, Wisconsin summers were scorchers.

One evening after a quiet supper with just Angel, Rags, and their mother, Mrs. O'Leary said, "Let's sit down in the living room before we do the dishes."

Her voice had a serious tone. She added,

"There is something I want to talk to you and Rags about."

Then it *was* serious. Her mother had had lots of time to talk at supper, but she'd only said things like "Pass the salad please, Rags," and "I hope we get that cool jet stream from the north that Dr. Walt (the weather man on Channel Five) has been predicting."

What was so important that she could not say it at the table? Was Rags in trouble? Was her mother ill? Had she, Angel, done something wrong?

"Sit there, Angel, on that soft chair. Rags, you sit beside me here on the couch."

Their mother was assigning them chairs! Like in school, in the principal's office! What in the world was the matter? Angel's mind raced over the last week. Were she and Rags eating too many candy bars? Drinking too much sugar-laden pop? Maybe her mother found that old denim skirt Angel had put in the trash. Angel had hated that skirt. Even if it was made over, it would not fit right.

"Now!" said their mother with what Angel thought was a sort of false gaiety in her voice. "You both know that the wedding is coming up in August!"

Angel had been trying to make her mother aware of that fact for ages! Now here she was, telling them something they knew very well for themselves!

Angel nodded politely. Rags was tracing the pattern of the floral couch with his finger.

"You know," their mother went on, "once we are married, Rudy will be your father."

Did their mother think they didn't know that? It had been in Angel's mind ever since the day they had green ham for dinner and Rudy had asked their mother to marry him. They had discussed this before, for goodness sake.

Angel nodded again, politely. Rags traced a particularly large flower all the way down the side of the couch to the floor.

"Sit up, Rags, and pay attention! You know," their mother went on, "being a father is not automatic. I mean, sometimes a mother gets married, and her new husband is *not* the father of the children.''

Now Angel frowned instead of nodding.

''Sometimes the natural father of the children remains the father even after the mother marries again. Then the mother's husband becomes the *step*father to the children.''

It sounded very confusing. A father is a father, thought Angel. Although she had to admit, Rudy would be a better father than most. She wondered if Rudy would expect them to call him ''Dad.'' It didn't feel natural to say ''Dad'' instead of ''Rudy.''

''What I'm getting at,'' her mother continued, ''is that Rudy wants to adopt you both.''

Now Angel was puzzled. Rags was emptying his pockets onto the arm of the couch. Where in the world had he gotten that rhinestone dog collar?

''He wants to be your *real* father, instead of your stepfather, because he loves you very much.''

"He *will* be our real father," said Rags, putting the dog collar around his own neck.

"No, Rags," said their mother.

"Uh *huh*," said Rags, defensively. "He will, *too*."

"In order for him to be your real father, he has to go to court and legally adopt you."

That would be very nice of Rudy, thought Angel, but she wondered why they had to discuss it if it was all decided.

"I wanted you to know, for several reasons," said Mrs. O'Leary. "And one of them is that it will mean some small changes."

Rags looked up, frowning. Angel said, "What changes?"

"Well, your name will change, for one thing," said her mother. "Mine will change too, when I marry, but ordinarily yours would remain the same. Rudy plans to adopt you right away, so after the wedding, we will all have his last name. He says it will make us more of a family. It would be confusing if, say, half of the family had one name, and half had another!"

Angel had not thought of names. She assumed (and wrongly, evidently) that once a person has a name, from babyhood on, it is your name forever. Unless of course you change it when you get married, but all the children she knew had certainly never changed their names. "Angel O'Leary" came out smoothly and with no thought, if someone said, "What is your name?" Her name was very close to her, she found to her surprise. She could not even imagine having another one!

"I want to be Burt!" said Rags. "Can I be Burt, Mom?"

Angel scoffed. Leave it to Rags to completely misunderstand.

"Not your first name, Rags," said their mother patiently. "Only your last name changes in adoption."

"I want to be Burt," pouted Rags, still wearing the dog collar. Angel's mother had once read Rags a story in which the character who was the detective was named Burt.

"Don't like Rags," he went on. "Want to be Burt."

"You can't be Burt!" shouted Angel, thinking how foolish Rags looked in a dog collar. Her brother was so — immature!

"Your name will be legally changed on all the records," their mother went on. "On your library card and the school records and at the dentist and doctor and all those things."

Angel didn't see what all the fuss was about. But then she remembered Rudy's last name!

Rudy had always been Rudy, since her mother met him, and the matter of his last name rarely came up. No one seemed to call him "Mister" — they just called him Rudy. But he did have a last name. And Angel remembered it now that it was on the verge of becoming her own name! It was a long name that Angel could not even pronounce. It was the longest name Angel had ever heard of!

Now Angel knew why her mother had called them here. This name change was no small thing! A person should be able to spell her own name! At the very least she had to be able to pronounce it!

"Do you know Rudy's last name?" said Mrs. O'Leary, cautiously.

Rags nodded. "Clown," he said. "Rudy Clown."

"No," she said, still patient. "Rudy *works* as a clown, Rags. That is not his last name."

Her mother looked at Angel.

"It's long," said Angel. "And it starts with a P."

"That's right!" said her mother, as if Angel had answered a test question correctly. "His name is Pappadopolis, and that will be your last name, too, in August!"

She said it as if it would be lots of fun to have a last name like Pappadopolis! Although Angel loved Rudy dearly, she did not share her mother's joy over a new last name. Especially one that sounded like the name of a city, or of some foreign hot dish one might have in a restaurant with candles burning in wicker-covered wine bottles. This *was* serious!

"It is a Greek name," said the smiling Mrs. O'Leary (soon to be Mrs. Pappadopolis).

"Greeky leaky," sang Rags in his dog collar. "Greeky leaky, Greeky leaky," he sang.

Their mother frowned.

Poor Rags, thought Angel. He had no idea of the trouble that was soon to befall him. Rags would enter kindergarten in the fall and would probably not be able even to *say* his name, and he

certainly would not be able to spell it or write
it! It had taken him ages to learn to write
"O'Leary"! He had practiced on old envelopes,
bits of paper, even on wet cement, with back-
ward letters and upside-down vowels. Angel
thought of the patience she and her mother had
practiced and the days of erasing and rewriting
they did until finally the day came when Rags did
it correctly. Now they were about to do the whole
thing all over again. And it would take Rags ages
to write his new name in school. People with the
names of Smith and Jones and even O'Leary
would finish much sooner and be chosen to wash
the blackboards and straighten chairs. Angel pic-
tured poor Rags at his desk long into the dark
night, the janitor asking him to lift his feet so he
could sweep under them and go home, too.

"Rudy's grandparents came to America from
Greece years ago," Mrs. O'Leary was saying.
"Rudy does not look Greek, because his mother
is Irish."

But Angel's mind was now on her monogrammed sweaters, so carefully hand-done for

her alone. There was no way an *L* could be turned into a *P*.

And what about her personalized stationery? It said, "A note from Angel" at the top, but the envelopes had her whole name and address on them. Wasted. They would have to be thrown away, or used as scrap paper.

"What about my stationery I got from Aunt Beth for Christmas?" said Angel, feeling as if she was losing her identity.

Her mother shrugged her shoulders. "We'll get new stationery," she said. "How important is a little paper?"

Well, it was important to Angel, Angel thought crossly. It said who she was, and now she wouldn't be that person anymore. Angel Pappadopolis. It was awful. It was worse than awful! It was long and awkward, but what was even worse: it was *funny*. People laughed at funny names. She could hear Peter Harris now.

"Popeye Angel, Poppy Doppy, Poppy Doppy!" he'd call.

Or worse yet, "Hey, Minneapolis! Indianapolis! Angel is a city!'' the boys would sing.

Her mother was still going on about Rudy's Greek heritage. When she was through, Angel's mind was spinning with worries. Her initials would be ''A.P.'' Just like the supermarket! There was an A&P down the street! She could hear Peter taunting, ''Hey, A.P.! Go get me some tuna fish, will ya?''

''And so, I just wanted to tell you about the name,'' their mother finished, putting her arms around their shoulders. Rags jumped up and was off like lightning to play. Angel wanted to ask questions, to say she wanted to keep her name, to hold on to her stationery and monograms.

But when her mother said, ''Is everything all right, Angel?'', Angel heard herself say, ''Sure.''

She surely did not want her mother to think she was ungrateful. Or that she did not like Rudy and appreciate being his daughter. No, it was something she would have to deal with privately. And she would have to deal with it soon — if she was going to get used to being a Pappadopolis by August!

8.
For the Worse, Not the Better

Angel went out and sat on the back porch steps, where she could think. She lined up in her mind all the negative things and all the positive things she could think of, about having a new last name. She could think of lots of negatives, but almost no positives. The only positive thing about a new name, she thought, would be if she wanted to be a criminal. A new name was a positive thing for a criminal, she supposed. It would be a chance for him to start over on a new life. A clean slate so to speak. When someone was looking for Henry Smith, he could say, "Oh, I'm Henry Williams," and escape safely.

But Angel had no plans to become a criminal.

And she could not think of another good thing about changing her name.

Suddenly Alyce drove up to the curb. She parked her car carefully and walked around to where Angel was sitting on the steps.

"What's troubling you?" she said with a smile, looking at the frown on Angel's face.

Angel did not want to discuss her problem with Alyce. But Alyce persisted. She sat down beside Angel on the step and said, "Before long we will be going to a wedding!"

At the mention of the word *wedding*, Angel's reserve gave way, and she cried, "I have to change my name! Rudy is adopting us!"

It took Alyce a few minutes to take all this in. When she did, she stood up and said, "Oh, that's not a problem. Now it would be different if Rudy's name was 'O'Malley' or 'Olsen.' "

"Why?" said Angel, wondering why in the world it mattered.

"Why, an 'O' name would mean bad luck for their marriage," she said in a confiding tone. She shook her head, and her finger, at Angel. "It

would be off to a bad start, mark my words. But
Pappadopolis now — that will work just fine."

Alyce continually puzzled Angel. When she
looked confused, Alyce bent over and whispered
into her ear in a secretive manner:

"Change your name and not the letter,
You marry for the worse, and not the better."

"You can just be glad Rudy's name does not

start with an *O*," she said in an all-knowing way. "Mark my words."

Alyce knocked at the back door and went in, calling, "Anyone home? Yoo hoo!"

"Come on in, Alyce." Angel could hear her mother call from some great distance, probably upstairs. Then her mother must have come down, because the voices became clearer.

There was talk of how warm it was and of the sale at the Big Store, and then Angel heard Alyce say, "Make sure you save July twelfth. That's the day of my shower for you."

"How exciting!" said Angel's mother. "That's very nice of you, Alyce, to go to all the work of having a bridal shower."

"It's the least I can do for a good friend," said Alyce warmly. "And I love planning a shower! I want Angel and Rags there too."

"I don't know about Rags," said Angel's mother with a frown in her voice. "He could get into some kind of shower trouble . . ."

Angel could almost see Alyce wave her mother's doubts away with a sweep of her hand. Alyce never anticipated trouble, Angel realized. She did not expect it and when it came it was always a surprise. But Angel knew that Rags was definitely not bridal shower material.

"He will love the games," Alyce said, as if reading Angel's mind. "Rags likes games." Alyce sounded final.

Mrs. O'Leary and Alyce went on talking of shower games and prizes and invitations. Edna approached Angel's house on her bike. She tied it to the fence, and gave it some make-believe hay. Then she climbed the steps and sat down beside Angel.

"Alyce is giving Mom a shower," said Angel.

"That will be fun," said Edna. "You might win a nice prize. Once I got a lingerie bag with lace on it. I keep my good underwear in it."

Angel kept her underwear in her underwear drawer. She could not see much sense in putting it into a bag when it was already in a drawer.

"Why?" she asked.

"You put a sachet in it and it makes it smell really good, like roses or lavender or something."

Angel's clothes smelled good already, because her mother used Cuddles fabric softener in the dryer.

"I've never been to a shower before," admitted Angel.

"I've been to lots," said Edna.

Somehow that did not surprise Angel. She might have known that Edna had been to showers. She'd been to everything. Angel sighed. There did not seem to be any experience that she could have before Edna, except the time when her mother went out of town. And even then, Edna seemed to end up more experienced than Angel.

But then Angel remembered something that had not happened to Edna. She had never had her name changed!

"Rudy is adopting us, and I am going to have a new name!" said Angel proudly. "I'll have to get all new monogrammed stuff."

Edna looked surprised but not envious. She might say she would not want to have a new name, but at least she could *not* say that it had already happened to her! She had the same name she was born with.

"That happened to my cousin," said Edna. "Her last name was Rossinelli, and when her dad died my aunt married a man named Ryan so she had to change her name to Ryan. Everyone got really mixed up."

"Are they real poor?" said Angel. "Or sick?"

"No, why should they be?"

So Alyce was wrong. She could not be trusted.

" 'Change your name and not the letter, you marry for the worse and not the better,' " recited Angel. She felt disgusted with Alyce's sayings.

"Well, Mr. Ryan does travel a lot. Sometimes they don't see him for a month at a time. My mom said she wouldn't want to live like that, with a husband who is never home. It's not good for the kids," she went on wisely.

Traveling *could* be for the worse instead of the better, Angel mused. It would be awful to have Rudy away for months at a time. Angel's own father had gone away, and that definitely was for the worse. Maybe Alyce knew what she was talking about, after all.

Edna had forgotten Rudy's last name. It had not seemed funny when it was just Rudy's name. But now that it was going to be Angel's name, it was. When Angel told her what it was, Edna roared.

"Pappadopolis!" she squealed. "It's so — *long!*"

"It's Greek," said Angel, defensively. "Rudy's grandparents are Greek."

"It reminds me of a city," Edna said with a snicker. "But we'll get used to it after a while," she added more kindly.

When it got dark, Edna left. Angel went into the house and to her room to get ready for bed. Her mind was spinning with names and monograms and bridal showers, and that night she dreamed about all the bad things that happened to her because her mother decided to marry a man with a plainer name, but one that started with *O*.

*   *   *

At last, signs of the upcoming wedding began to appear. Rudy began moving some of his things into the house, ahead of time. One or two early wedding presents arrived and were placed on a card table in the living room. Thank-you notes were on the dining room table along with stamps and pens. Ads came for their mother for half off on a subscription to *Modern Bride,* and a twenty percent discount on a Caribbean cruise. The car finally went into the shop to be repainted and Mrs. O'Leary put dates on the calendar for a shopping trip for wedding clothes for Angel and Rags. Also on the calendar, Angel noticed, were large *X*s drawn through every passing day, and there was a big red circle around the August wedding date with an exclamation mark through it. Their mother was counting the days till the wedding, even though she did not seem to be doing a lot of planning.

There were several parties with people from her mother's office, but Rudy and Angel's mother went to those alone. And then, very quickly it seemed, the day of Alyce's shower arrived.

9.
The Rabbit at the Bridal Shower

Rudy drove Angel and Rags and Mrs. O'Leary to Alyce's house at two o'clock. Then he was going to the television station to do some work, since Alyce had said that men do not come to bridal showers.

"Then why am I coming?" sulked Rags. "I'm not a girl."

"You're not a man," said Angel. "You're a boy."

That seemed to settle it. Rags could not argue about that. Rudy was a man and Rags wasn't. Angel and Rags had small packages under their arms for their mother, although Alyce had made it clear that, since they were "family," a gift was not necessary. Angel told Rags it would not look right if they were the only ones there with no gifts, so Angel got her mother a box of her favorite candy, and Rags brought some baseball cards that he said would be very valuable someday in case his mother got very poor and needed to sell them to buy food.

"Some even have the gum still in them," he said proudly.

When Rags told Angel about how their mother could sell them, she was reminded again of Alyce's words, "Marry for the worse and not the better." Why did Alyce's words keep coming back to her, haunting words that repeated themselves in some back corner of her mind?

When they got out of the car at the curb, they could see a large sign across the front of Alyce's door: SOMEONE'S GETTING MARRIED! Rudy laughed, and Mrs. O'Leary blushed.

"People can see it from a block away!" she said.

"The guests won't go to the wrong house!" said Rudy cheerfully. Rudy always seemed to see the bright side of any situation. He reminded Angel of someone in a book she'd read — who was that? — Pollyanna! It was an old, old book about a girl with a good deal of misfortune. She was an orphan, Angel remembered. But no matter what happened to her, she made the best of it.

Rudy waved and drove off and the children and their mother knocked at Alyce's door. Angel did not have a clear idea of what to expect of this shower, but whatever it was, it was not what she saw before her when Alyce threw open the door, singing, "Here is our guest of honor now!" Angel's mouth fell open and Rags stared and their mother looked as if she would laugh out loud. Alyce was dressed as a Christmas tree! She was all green, and covered with ornaments and tinsel. Pine branches sloped down her shoulders and arms, on her ears were red bells, and atop her head was a star. But the most astounding thing of all, was that Alyce *twinkled*! Tiny lights all over her body went on and off cheerfully. Lights of many different colors.

"Are we at a Christmas party, instead of a shower?" said Mrs. O'Leary.

Angel found herself looking over her shoulder to be sure the grass was green, and not covered with snow.

"Our shower has a holiday theme!" said Alyce, still twinkling. "Everyone has come as a different holiday, and brought a gift for that season! I myself am Father Christmas!"

Angel thought to herself, of course, Alyce could not have a normal shower! A shower with an umbrella hanging upside down filled with gifts, such as Edna had talked about. Everything about Alyce had a theme. Alyce loved themes.

"Bubba!" shouted Rags, running after Alyce's dog, who was wearing some sort of plastic antlers, and had his nose painted red for the occasion.

"Bubba is Rudolph today!" said Alyce. Angel noticed that even the cat and the canary cage had red ribbons tied to them.

Milling about the room in the background, Angel saw Christopher Columbus, Father Time, a plump pilgrim, and a construction worker in a hard yellow hat.

"She's Labor Day," said Alyce, when she saw Angel's puzzled look. "Now, first of all," she continued, holding up her branches for silence, "we will get into the spirit of things by singing a few Christmas songs!"

Angel thought everyone looked as if they were in the spirit of things already, but Alyce was passing out Christmas song books and shouting, "Page five, everyone!"

Angel's mother sat in a festively decorated chair, and piled all around her were holiday-wrapped gifts. Everyone joined in singing "Deck the Halls" and "Rudolph" and "Jolly Old St. Nicholas," while Rags chased Bubba between chairs and around tables. They continued the chase until Alyce stopped twinkling.

"My extension cord!" she shouted. Alyce's long extension cord had come out of the socket and was tangled around Bubba's neck. He ran under tables and into the kitchen, pulling Alyce and her ornaments along with him.

"Get him!" shouted a large Easter Bunny.

Angel and Rags tore after Bubba and pulled him out from under the kitchen table.

"Bad dog!" scolded Rags.

"Bad reindeer!" laughed Angel.

The children untangled Alyce's wires and plugged her in again, and she began twinkling as before.

"Now that we're all in the spirit, we will play our shower games," announced Alyce.

She passed out paper and pencils to all the guests.

"This is called a cake game!" she announced. "I will read a description, and you write down what kind of cake I'm describing."

Alyce called out "A cake for a thin person." Angel knew the answer. She wrote down "Pound Cake" on the top line. Rags whined that he did not know the answer. Angel wondered if it would be cheating to help him. Poor Rags would not win any game — he was too young to know about cakes!

"A cake for a painter," Alyce was calling.

There were many puzzled faces. Christopher Columbus frowned.

Angel wrote down, "Rainbow."

"Cake for a bad person" was easy. Devil's Food. And of course "a heavenly cake" would be Angel Food. But when Alyce called "A cake for a banker," Angel was stumped. The Easter Bunny wrote something down without hesitation. There were ten more kinds of cakes, and Angel knew only five of them. Rags had given up and was poking his finger in Clarence's cage.

Alyce collected the papers in an orderly manner, Angel thought, very much like a teacher in school. She took some moments to look them over, and then announced that Angel's own mother was the winner!

"Angel did very well, too," said Alyce, just as her teacher did in school to encourage those who tried. "Margaret Toomer came in second, but she missed the cake for a statue."

Angel wondered what in the world a cake for a statue could be. She glanced at her mother's winning paper. It said, "Marble." Her mother certainly knew her cakes. But then she had been baking birthday cakes for years and years. Mrs. O'Leary opened her prize. It was a cake cookbook.

"Now, wasn't that *fun!*" said Alyce, twinkling and smiling at the same time. Angel thought she would look even nicer after dark, with the room lights out.

Alyce was passing out more paper now. The paper had mixed-up letters on it, like XIMRE and VOTES. Angel loved word games. Alyce was telling everyone to unscramble the letters and make words for kitchen appliances. This time Rags didn't even try to win. He walked over to the table where the food was put out, covered with plastic wrap and foil, waiting for the shower luncheon. He played his own game, guessing what was under the foil wrap.

Alyce gave everyone only five minutes to unscramble the words. That was all that Angel needed. She found she was having a good time at this shower. It was almost like a good day at school. She wrote "mixer" and "stove" and went on to unscramble "blender" and "skillet" and "roaster." When Alyce blew her whistle and said, "Time's up," Margaret Toomer said, "I only have three of them!" And Angel's mother had only eight. "That 'VOTES' stopped me," she said.

"That's 'stove,'" said Angel, anxious for Alyce to correct the papers.

"Angel won!" shouted Alyce. "Angel was the only one who got them all!"

She came toward Angel with a box wrapped festively in red and white paper. Angel opened it and found — an electric can opener! Alyce did stick to a theme. A cake book for a cake game. An appliance for an appliance game!

"It's for your hope chest," said Alyce. "You put it away till you are married."

"Or until you have an apartment of your own," added Angel's mother. "You don't have to be married to use a can opener."

Angel was relieved to hear her mother say that. It might be a long time before she was married. The can opener could rust by then.

A few more games were played, and then Rags said, "I want to win! Don't I win anything?"

"You'll win our last game," said Alyce confidently. Angel wondered how Alyce knew he would win. Angel herself felt she would cheat if she had to, to see that Rags won at something. It was no fun not winning at any game, being almost the only one without a prize.

Alyce uncovered the plates on the table. She told everyone to take a good look at the table and the food for five minutes. Then they all had to turn their backs on the table and answer questions Alyce asked.

"How many brownies are on the blue plate?" said Alyce. While everyone else was thinking, Rags shouted, "Ten!"

"Good!" said Alyce. She wrote down one point for Rags.

"Now, what is in the round silver bowl at the end of the table?"

Rags waved his hand wildly. "Peanuts!" he said.

"Two points for Rags!" cried Alyce.

Rags also knew exactly how many heart-shaped sandwiches there were, and how many wedding bells. The only one he missed was what was sprinkled on the fondue.

"But that wasn't fair because I don't know what fondue is!" he cried.

"Rags is right. That was not fair. And he did get more right than anyone else," Alyce added.

Of course, thought Angel. Who else would count sandwiches and study bowls of candy? But Angel was very glad Rags won honestly and didn't have to be given a booby prize, or a prize out of pity. That would have been humiliating.

"Do you know why I won?" Rags was saying, standing in front of the whole group with pride. "I counted the *uncovered* things before the game! I knew what everything was even before we played."

Angel hoped that would not be considered cheating, or taking unfair advantage. Why didn't Rags keep quiet about how he did it? She had heard Alyce say once: "Don't fix it if it works!" That was it. Leave it alone if you win!

But no one seemed to think Rags had won unfairly, and Alyce handed him a box that rattled. It was filled with peanuts and colored mints and chocolate-covered raisins — all things that Rags loved!

Mrs. O'Leary whispered to Rags to save his prize until he got home, and put it beside her for safekeeping. Angel was relieved, remembering how Rags had overeaten at parties in the past and been sick before they were over.

"Now!" said Alyce, clapping her branches together. "What we have all been waiting for! It's time for the bride to open her gifts!"

"It *is* like Christmas!" said Mrs. O'Leary, with her arms around Angel and Rags.

"Rags can cut the ribbon and help you open the tape," Alyce was saying, bustling about getting a pair of scissors, "and Angel can make a bouquet out of the ribbons!"

As Alyce had said, the gifts had a holiday theme. There was a calendar-diary from Father Time, and green napkins and placemats from St. Patrick. There was a croquet set from the Fourth of July, and a carving set from Thanksgiving. Angel wondered what the "Christmas" gift would be from Alyce! But they got to the bottom of the huge pile, and there had been nothing with Alyce's name on it!

"Oh, dear me!" said Alyce. "I forgot to take my gift out of the freezer! I wanted to wait until the last minute, and I waited too long!" She went dashing out of the room, her extension cord trailing. When she returned, she was carrying a very, very large turkey, wrapped only in its freezer wrap of plastic and yellow netting!

"I didn't get it wrapped!" said Alyce, out of breath, and looking penitent. The guests were laughing and Mrs. O'Leary gave Alyce a hug and said, "This will be our very first Christmas dinner together, and you all must come! It's large enough to feed an army!"

Alyce announced that it was time to eat, and everyone formed a line at the table, with Mrs. O'Leary and Angel and Rags at the head of it. Angel took several heart-shaped sandwiches and two wedding bells. There was also fruit salad and chicken salad, and sugar cookies in the shape of love birds.

"What a good party, Alyce!" said Rags. Everyone agreed that it was a splendid party.

"Rudy will come and pick us up," said Angel's mother. "And it's a good thing, with all of the gifts we have to take home!"

Mrs. O'Leary went to call Rudy on the telephone, to tell him they were almost ready, but when she came back she was frowning.

"He doesn't answer, at home or at the station," she said.

"Oh, he's probably having a coffee break at the diner," said Alyce.

"How come there are two Easter Bunnies?" Rags said.

Everyone stopped eating and looked up, their forks poised in midair. Sure enough, at the buffet table was another large rabbit, helping himself to heart-shaped sandwiches and fruit salad. The rabbit sat down on a chair in the corner and began to eat.

"Who could it be?" murmured Margaret Toomer.

"I don't recognize that rabbit," said Alyce thoughtfully.

In a few moments the strange rabbit got up, tripped over a chair leg, and fell. Instead of getting up, he turned somersaults across the room, and then got up and walked to the table and began juggling paper plates over his head.

"Rudy!" shouted Rags, running up to him and throwing his arms around his legs.

The rabbit smiled. "I came to help clean up," he said. Before he did that, he did some more tricks for the shower audience, and then led them in another sing-along at Alyce's piano. Only this time they sang funny songs, songs like "Itsy Bitsy Spider" that Rags could act out.

Then, after the guests left, Rudy helped put Alyce's apartment back in order, and they all untrimmed her and packed her lights and ornaments away. Then they loaded the gifts in the back of the car and said good-bye.

"It was a wonderful party," said Mrs. O'Leary.

"How did you know the theme of the shower?" whispered Angel to Rudy, in the car.

"Theme?" said Rudy. "What theme? I find my rabbit ears are suitable for all occasions!"

"You're a rabbit for all seasons," said Mrs. O'Leary.

10.
Closer to the Wedding

As the day of the wedding grew closer and closer, Angel noticed that her mother began making more preparations in earnest. She said things like, "I hope the asters and mums will be blooming in time," or "I hope they won't be *through* blooming by that time." She talked on the phone to the local minister, and asked Rudy if he planned to wear the suit he had or get a new one. When he said, "The suit I have," she said, "Then it had better go to the cleaners."

The more her mother prepared, the less Angel worried. At last her mother was *doing* something. No doubt she had found out that Edna had been right: there were things you had to do to get

ready for a wedding. No matter how small, weddings needed preparation. And even though no
formal invitations were sent out, people were
coming and needed a place to stay. Rudy's parents would be flying in, and his aunt with them.
And when Rudy's clown friends found out about
the wedding, they decided they must be there, all
together, in a group.

This presented a brand-new worry for Angel.
Clowns were known as jokers — would they
show up in clown suits? Angel remembered when
Rudy first came to Elm City — she had had that
same worry. But he had worn regular clothes and
looked respectable. However, there was no telling what his friends were like. They might think
it would be hilarious to appear in costume.

And Angel still worried about her name
change. She dreaded the day she would write
"Angel Pappadopolis" on her school assign-
ments. But so much was happening on those last
August days that there was hardly any time to
worry about either of those problems at any
length. When she began to worry, her mother

would say, "Did you see my address book, Angel?" or Rudy would ask for a stamp, or Rags would pull on her sleeve and ask help for something. So she just put off worrying until later.

Mrs. O'Leary had so many things to put on lists that she began carrying a pencil behind her ear. One morning she looked at that list and said, "We have to get you a new dress for the wedding, Angel!"

It was agreed that Angel was too old to be a flower girl and too young to be a bridesmaid, but her mother said she could be a junior bridesmaid and wear a dress that was not too fancy — something she could wear later for parties, and for Sundays.

"This is a small wedding," her mother kept saying. "Alyce will be the maid of honor, you will be the junior bridesmaid, and Rags will be the ring bearer. But it will be very informal. No long dresses."

Mrs. O'Leary herself had said she would wear something she "had in her closet." But as the day got closer, she decided she should have a new dress. "After all," she said, "a person doesn't get married every day."

"I hope not!" Rudy said, in mock horror. "I think a wedding at least deserves a new dress!"

"But just a simple one," Angel's mother said. "Today is the day. I think we should go to the city and look for something suitable for Rags, and for you and me, Angel."

Angel's mother phoned Alyce and asked her if she wanted to come along and look for a dress for the wedding, too, but Alyce said she was busy housecleaning and would go to the city by herself next week and choose her dress.

"Just something simple," said Mrs. O'Leary. "Maybe a nice pastel shade."

When Angel heard her mother tell Alyce "something simple," she had a third worry. Did Alyce know what "simple" meant? Would Alyce come in something fancier than the bride wore?

"Don't you think you should help Alyce choose a dress?" said Angel to her mother. "What if it has a bunch of ruffles, or a hoop or something?"

Mrs. O'Leary frowned. "Well, she can't go today, and I can't go next week," she said. "I think we can trust Alyce to choose something tasteful . . ." Even as her mother said the words, Angel knew she, too, must have some doubts about leaving Alyce on her own, shopping. "I mean, she *is* a full-grown woman," said Mrs. O'Leary sensibly. And then Rudy honked the horn at the curb and called for them to leave for the city. Mrs. O'Leary forgot about Alyce and her dress, and ran to comb Rags's hair and get her purse. Angel did not forget it but stored it in the back of her mind with her other problems.

Angel and Rags sat in the back seat of the car on the way to the city, and Rudy and Angel's mother, in the front seat, discussed asking Margaret Toomer to sing.

"We really should have organ music, but the piano will have to do," said her mother.

"What does a ring bear do?" said Rags to Angel, as they rode along.

"You carry the wedding ring on a little pil-low," said Angel.

Rags frowned. He wondered why he would have to dress as a bear to do that. He remembered what Angel had told him about "tradition" and customs and began to look forward to being a bear. "Why don't you be a fox?" asked Rags.

Angel was deep in thoughts of new dresses and bouquets and said, "Don't talk silly, Rags. Grow up."

If Angel thought it was silly to be ring fox, that

was all right. He would be a ring bear all alone. It would be more fun that way, anyway. Everyone would surely watch him. A ring bear would stand out at a wedding.

At last they came to the city and Rudy drove to the mall and parked the car. They began at one end of the mall, and went into all of the dress shops. After two hours had passed and they hadn't found anything suitable, Rudy said they should stop for lunch. Rags was getting fussy, and even Rudy's humor and a chocolate milk shake did not cheer him. Angel herself was not enjoying the shopping as much as she thought she would, because neither she nor her mother seemed to find the kind of dresses they wanted. Even in the children's stores, Mrs. O'Leary did not find anything Rags could wear.

At the end of the afternoon, she said, "I'm going to have to order Rags's suit from the catalog. Nothing in this whole mall is right."

"Not one bear suit," Rags sang under his breath. "I didn't see one bear suit."

"What's that, Rags?" said his mother.

"No suit for a ring bear," he repeated. "Not even one."

"We'll order one from the catalog," she said warmly. "Don't worry, Rags, by next week we will have one that is just right. I'll measure you and they will send one in just your size."

"Good," said Rags. Since he had been chosen to be the bear, he would not like to have things fall through. He could not remember seeing bear suits in the catalog at home, though, just shorts and T-shirts and shoes and socks and some long pants and dress shirts with little bow ties that almost no one Rags knew ever wore. But if his mother said they had bear suits, they must have them.

Once that was decided, Rudy took Rags off to the petting zoo in the mall, and Angel and her mother tried the last store in the mall for dresses.

"Look!" said Angel's mother. "That dress on the model! That is just the dress I am looking for."

Angel agreed, it was a wonderful dress. It was a bluish color her mother called "teal" and was not too plain and not too fancy. It looked exactly right. And they had her size! When Mrs. O'Leary put the dress on, it fit her perfectly, and Angel said, "It is a perfect dress to get married in. If you don't want to have a long white dress with a veil," she added.

Mrs. O'Leary was so happy and relieved, she gave Angel a big hug and paid for the dress and said, "Now, if only we can find *your* dress, Angel, we will be all set!"

Set except for Alyce's dress, thought Angel. But Mrs. O'Leary was heading to the children's section and had no worries about Alyce's choice.

Mrs. O'Leary browsed through the racks of dresses in Angel's size, and suddenly said, "Here! Look at this, Angel! Do you like this one?" She held up a pretty pale-lavender dress on its hanger.

It was another perfect dress, not too fancy, but not too plain. It looked just right for a junior bridesmaid who was in a small wedding and who wanted to wear the dress later for Sundays or a party.

"I like it," said Angel, who thought maybe she would have said that anyway because she was so tired of the mall and the noise and the rows and rows of stiff bright colors. She tried the dress on and her mother said, "Angel, you look beautiful! We'll get a matching hair ribbon and socks and you will really look like an angel!"

Angel smiled at her mother's joke and began to feel excited about the wedding day. For so long it had been barely real, but now that she had a pretty dress for the occasion it meant it would really happen — her mother was getting married. She and Rags were going to have their own father. A nice father. A clown for a father!

Her mother paid for the dress and with two dresses, each in its own box, Angel and her mother started in the direction of the petting zoo to find Rags and Rudy. Right outside the zoo, on a wooden bench, they saw them. Rags was sleeping peacefully beside Rudy, and Rudy was doing a crossword puzzle in a newspaper. His face lit up in a smile when he saw them. Rudy never seemed to get tired, Angel thought.

"I see boxes!" he said. "You found wedding dresses!"

Angel's mother told Rudy excitedly about their finds. "But you can't see them till the wedding!" she added. "It would be bad luck."

Angel filed that in the back of her mind. It was something (surprisingly) that Edna had not mentioned. Seeing wedding dresses before the wedding was bad luck. There seemed to be many, many omens connected with bad luck at weddings! Angel wondered why there were no *good* luck omens. No one yet had told her a good luck story.

Rudy picked Rags up carefully and carried him to the car. Feeling satisfied with a good shopping day, they started home. Rags was soon wide awake and in a good mood. He sat in his corner of the car humming one of his favorite songs. But his thoughts were not on the song, or the scenery, or his mother's purchases for the day. His thoughts were on ring bears. No one seemed interested in telling him exactly what a ring bear did at the wedding, besides carry the little pillow with the ring. There must be something else. Otherwise why have a *bear* do it? Anyone at all could carry a ring on a pillow. Rudy himself could put it into his coat pocket!

No, if a bear was to do it, there must be some bear-like quality needed. And if no one told him what it was, Rags would have to think of it himself. Hadn't his mother always said he was creative? He felt sure his mother wanted him to take on the bear job on his own.

11.
New Worries

Margaret Toomer agreed to sing, and Angel's mother put a check after that item on her list. She took Rudy's suit to the cleaners, and she bought a satin hair ribbon the color of Angel's dress. She ordered a suit for Rags to be ring bearer in, a simple suit that could (like Angel's dress) be worn at other times. She reminded Alyce that she should get a simple dress — one that she could wear after the wedding as well.

Angel felt weights lifted from her shoulders since her mother had sprung into action. She only worried now about Alyce's understanding "simple" (Alyce who could easily come lit up with twinkling lights), Rudy's clown friends coming

in proper attire, and, of course, the more perma-
nent worry of her last name. That seemed too big
even to dream of solving.

Rooms were cleaned and cots set up upstairs to
accommodate the overnight guests. Rags and
Angel's own grandma was coming, and Rudy's
parents, and they would all stay in the house with
them. Rudy's clown friends would stay in a ho-
tel. Furniture was moved in and out of the living
room and a place decided on for the ceremony.

"I think it should be in front of the artificial
fireplace," said Angel. "Then the people can sit
facing the staircase and see us coming down the
steps."

"Isn't that a bit Hollywoodish?" said Angel's
mother. "Remember, this is a small, informal
wedding."

"That sounds fine to me," said Rudy, when
consulted. "I think all brides and junior bridesmaids and ring bearers should come down a stair-
way."

Rudy was so understanding! Angel had a feeling he was a nicer father than most.

Wedding gifts began to pour in. The house took on a very festive air, with ribbons, tissue paper, and the white excelsior packing material that cradled silver candlesticks and crystal pickle dishes.

"Who is *this* from?" asked Edna one morning. Edna came daily to see what new things had arrived. She pointed to a large bowl with a statue that seemed to grow out of the middle of it.

"That is a punch bowl," Angel explained. "You put punch in it, and it turns into a fountain. The punch comes out of the statue's umbrella. You know, like it's raining punch."

Edna stared at it.

"It lights up, too, when you plug it in. You turn the lights out at night and all you see is this colored punch coming out of the fountain."

"Who is it from?" Edna repeated.

"Alyce," said Angel.

Edna began to laugh. "Alyce's gifts are — unusual," she said. "A turkey, and a lit-up punch bowl!"

The lit-up punch bowl reminded Angel of the

lit-up Christmas tree, and the lit-up tree reminded her of clothes, and clothes reminded her that Alyce was choosing her dress by herself.

"Isn't it romantic," said Edna. "A wedding right here in your own house."

Leave it to Edna to talk about romance — something else Angel was not familiar with.

"I'd like to get married in a living room," Edna mused. "It's so — private."

"I think churches are better," said Angel, who

had not really given it any thought until now.

"Where are they going on their honeymoon?" demanded Edna.

Angel had not thought about honeymoons any more than she'd thought about churches. "I don't know," she said.

"That's so romantic, having your mother go on a honeymoon."

"It's just a small wedding," said Angel, feeling called upon to downplay romance. A person's mother should not be romantic. A mother should be practical, and a good shopper.

Edna's eyes looked dreamy. Angel thought Edna was being even more imaginative than Angel herself was. Movie stars had romances. Not mothers, or people you knew. Edna had a wild imagination, thinking Angel's mother would have a romantic honeymoon.

"My mom and Rudy are not romantic," said Angel.

"Of course they are. They're in love, aren't they?"

"You see too many movies," said Angel.

"Well, they *are* in love, you know," said Edna. "Why else would they be getting married?"

Angel started to say, "So Rags and I will have a father," but she stopped. She knew that was not true. If that was true, then her mother could have married anyone before this. Could Edna be right? Could her mother be "in love," like people on the afternoon soap operas? Surely that would not happen to a person's own mother. All that kissing and — well, it was true Rudy hugged her mother sometimes, but he hugged her and Rags, too!

"They will want to be alone," said Edna wisely, rolling her eyes knowingly. "They won't want you around after the wedding, you know. Brides and bridegrooms like to be alone."

Only in the movies, thought Angel. Surely mothers did not want to leave their children (again) when they just had become a family! And why? What would they do all day without her and Rags to take care of? Her mother herself had told her that children made everything you did more fun. She told Edna this.

"Not *everything*," said Edna mysteriously. "Not honeymoons."

Angel was again torn between being amazed at Edna's superior knowledge, and being troubled by it. It always gave her new things to worry about that she would not have to worry about if Edna had not told her.

Mrs. O'Leary walked into the room, a pencil behind her ear, a note pad in her hand, and a worried look on her face.

"Are you going on a honeymoon?" said Angel.

Her mother appeared to blush. She *was* "in love"!

"Just a short one," she said.

Oh no, thought Angel, Alyce will be here again! Alyce and her dress form and her animals and her relatives!

"One of Rudy's friends has a little cottage up north — we'll just go there for a few days, not long. Just a chance to get away after all the hassle of the wedding, and be alone for a bit.''

So that is what they were, hassle! She and Rags and the simple wedding!

Edna looked smug. Angel hated that look.

When Angel looked downcast, her mother said, ''It's just for a few days, Angel. It is best to begin a new life away, not right here where we have been living before Rudy came. And Margaret Toomer has agreed to stay with you and Rags.''

Margaret Toomer, who left town the last time she was needed! And what was the matter with their lovely old home, to start a marriage in?

Now that Edna had caused enough trouble, she said, ''Well, I'd better be going. My mom and dad and I are going to the city to a play.''

Lucky Edna. To be going *with* her parents — parents who were not ''in love.'' Who were not romantic. Who wanted to be with their daughter, and stay in their own home!

Angel sat down on the back steps after Edna left and realized her mother would not have grandchildren. Surely Rags was too flighty. And she, Angel, would never live long enough to have children. Just the other night on TV they had said that people who worry a lot and are overcome with emotional problems have a short life. The stress, it seemed, made you "type A," and that was dangerous. Well, Angel was surely "type A." Her life was full of stress and worry. Before one problem was solved another crisis came along to trouble her. She did not notice Edna ever worrying. How could she know so much and be so serene? Why didn't these things bother her? No doubt *her* parents would have tons of grandchildren.

Angel heard Rags inside, talking to his mother as she packed the honeymoon sheets.

"Did my ring bear suit come?" he asked.

"Not yet, Rags. But it will be here by next week, don't worry."

Don't worry. Don't worry. A lot of good those empty words did. But Rags seemed able to do just that. He ran off, singing and happy and trusting. Not worrying, just like Edna.

However, Rags *did* have worries, although Angel didn't see them. He was worrying about acting like a proper bear. He went to the bookshelf and took out his animal book and turned to the circus chapter. It was filled with bears. He looked at the bears in the colored rings. One was dancing. It had a hoop around its neck like a sort of collar. He tried to think of bears he had seen at the circus. What did they do? He knew they usually walked on all fours. Would that be enough? That was what an ordinary bear did. But a ring bear surely should do something special. A trick or two. He would do what Alyce had said to do once when you couldn't think of something right away. She said, "Sleep on it!" Rags would sleep on it. When he got up in the morning, he would know.

12.
Angel's Mother's Wedding!

On the day before the wedding, Rags's ring bearer suit had not arrived, and Rudy's suit had not come back from the cleaners. When Mrs. O'Leary called the cleaners, they assured her it would be ready first thing in the morning. When she called the catalog company, they said they had made an error and would send the suit overnight express.

"It will be there before ten!" said the man cheerfully.

"I hope so," said Mrs. O'Leary, picturing Rags wearing his overalls to the wedding.

The mums and asters that Angel's mother waited for were not at their best, and Rudy called the floral shop. "We need nice flowers," he said. "These look a little wilted."

The floral shop was to bring the flowers in the morning, but the night before they came with white runners and vases and green plants that were placed in the living room in readiness. Also on the night before the wedding, the children's grandma arrived. More last-minute gifts arrived, the cake was placed on a special table, and folding tables and chairs were unfolded and set up. The guests would be served at the wedding reception directly after the wedding.

Amid all of the excitement, Mrs. O'Leary could be heard saying, "This is just a small wedding . . ." but her words would trail off, and no one really believed her. It did not look like a small wedding.

At seven o'clock the minister came by to meet Rudy. Then Rudy left for the airport to pick up his parents from Washington, D.C. The house seemed to Angel and Rags to be filled with people and excitement — even more than Christmas or birthday parties. Rags was crawling around on all fours like some animal, under tables and around vases, and could be heard to growl. Every now and then his mother would say, "What are you doing down there on the floor, Rags?" or "Get up, Rags, and act your age." But then she would be distracted by some task and forget about Rags. His grandma tried to hold him on her lap and read him a story, but the excitement of the wedding made Rags what his mother called "hyper," and he could not sit still very long.

At ten o'clock Rudy arrived with his parents and his aunt, and they swept Angel and Rags up in their arms, and took out presents for them to open from their bags.

"Oooooo," squealed Rags. "A dump truck!"

"What a good gift for Rags!" exclaimed his mother. "Rags loves to haul dirt!" Angel wondered how their new grandparents knew Rags dug cities.

Angel opened her box, which was larger and more square, and she found a hand-carved music box inside!

"It is from Greece," said Rudy's mother, proudly.

"Wind it up," shouted Rags.

Angel did, and it played a tinkling, lively song, which Rudy said was a scarf dance.

Angel had never had a music box before, and she wondered if she should give this grandma-to-be a hug. But she felt a little shy, so instead she just said, "Thank you very much. It will be real pretty on my dresser."

"You're welcome," said her new grandparents, and Rudy's aunt came over and gave Angel a hug.

Then Rudy passed around a Greek drink called ouzo, which smelled to Angel like licorice, and after that they all went to The Gourmet for dinner.

Angel had never had dinner at ten-thirty at night before. Rags could hardly keep awake until dessert.

Wedding guests slept in Angel's room. Angel slept on the couch between the wedding gifts and a large potted rubber plant. Her mind was spinning. She tried to imagine what life would be like tonight without the wedding, without Rudy, without new loving grandparents. Just a simple thing like her mother having a boyfriend had so much more to it! Angel loved to play her "What if . . ." game all alone. What if they had not met Rudy? What if there were no wedding? Angel would be up in her little room alone, no gifts, no flowers, no white runners, no new grandparents, no honeymoon! Angel shivered. She was very glad her mother had taken that trip with Aunt Beth. She was sorry that Aunt Beth could not even be here now, the one who really should be here of all people, but she had called to say that she had a very important meeting that she could not miss, in Kentucky of all places, but that she would come to visit on her way home, when her sister and new brother-in-law had returned from their honeymoon. Maybe, thought Angel, Aunt Beth felt bad that she was not the one that Rudy had chosen to marry! What if Aunt Beth had liked Rudy herself?

In the morning very early the phone began ringing and ringing. Angel sat up on the couch

and said, "It is here. Today is my mother's wedding day!" Now the doorbell was ringing too!
Rudy announced fresh sweet rolls from the bakery for breakfast.

"Where's my ring bear suit?" whined Rags,
rubbing his sleepy eyes.

"It will be here by ten," said his mother. "It
is Rudy's suit we must check on now."

Rudy snapped his fingers and went to the
phone.

"There's no answer," he said, with a puzzled
look on his face. "The cleaners don't answer."

"They said they would deliver it," said Mrs.
O'Leary. "It's probably on the truck."

Rudy frowned.

After breakfast everyone had tasks to do, and
Angel and her mother went to the beauty parlor
to have their hair washed and curled. When they
came out, Angel thought neither of them looked
like herself — the hair that circled their faces was
just a little bit too curly, like the hair of someone
advertising shampoo on TV she thought. Her
mother seemed pleased, though, so perhaps that

is the way hair was supposed to look in a wedding. Surely Angel would not know. As Edna had made very clear, Angel was not familiar with weddings at all.

When they got home, Rags was sulking among the wedding gifts. When he saw Angel and his mother, his sulking turned to sobs. Beside him was a box with his ring bearer suit in it.

"It came!" said his mother. "Your ring bearer suit came!"

Rags cried even louder. "It *isn't* a ring bear suit!"

"Why, Rags," said his mother, "it looks just right! Let's try it on."

"It's just pants," sobbed Rags. "It hasn't even got fur."

"Stop talking nonsense," said his mother. "Let's see if it fits."

"There's no paws or head or anything," cried Rags.

"Grow up, Rags," said Angel in disgust. Rags could act terribly silly for someone who was about to start kindergarten in the fall. She often mentioned Rags's immaturity to her mother, saying, "He should have gone to nursery school. He is such a baby."

Their mother had to struggle to try the suit on Rags, and Angel said, "Tears are going to make stains all over it!"

"It's fine," their mother added. "It fits just right! I don't know what in the world you are crying about, Rags!"

Usually she would have pursued the cause of Rags's troubled feelings, but today she had too much on her mind. Rags sat on the edge of the bed, still sniffling, and wondering how he could be a ring bear without a bear suit. He would just have to play the part without a costume, he thought. It would have to be enough to simply *act* like a bear — he would do his best, and if no one knew he was a ring bear, well, it was his own mother's fault. She wanted a ring bear at her wedding, and then ordered him an ordinary store suit. She had only herself to blame if he looked human.

While Rags was brooding, Rudy stuck his head

in the door and said "The cleaner is closed."

"They will deliver," said Angel's mother confidently.

Rudy looked doubtful. "The truck is in front of the store," he said. "And no one is in it."

Now Mrs. O'Leary looked worried. "It's Saturday," she said. "They could be closed on Saturday, but they did say the suit would be here. I think we should be patient."

What else could they do, thought Angel. It was too late to drive to the city, and Elm City had no men's clothing stores. In fact, there was only one cleaner.

"Okay," said Rudy, who never believed in worrying if he didn't have to.

The time of the wedding drew closer. Baths were taken, and the florist truck arrived. Fresh flowers were placed all over the living room. The white runners were put down. The waiting chairs stood in rows. To Angel, it felt like a mixture of Christmas and the time she was in a school play in second grade. Her three grandparents helped her dress, her mother sprayed some perfume on her wrists, and downstairs she could hear Margaret at the piano, practicing a few strains of the Wedding March! The time drew closer and closer! People were beginning to come and sit in the folding chairs. When Angel looked over the banister, she saw Edna, who had curls, too, and her very best pink organdy dress on! Angel felt more nervous than ever.

And then from the front window, Angel saw a car drive up with Rudy's clown friends! There were six of them all together. And they were wearing perfectly normal clothes! No big shoes or floppy hats or rubber flowers that squirted water! Angel felt a surge of relief, seeing them walk sedately up the sidewalk, and in her mind she checked off one thing she did not have to worry about anymore.

Several people tried to come upstairs to talk to Angel's mother before the ceremony, but Margaret Toomer (who was at the bottom of the steps now) held up her hand. "It's bad luck to see the bride before the wedding," she said. "Especially the groom," she said, looking at

Rudy. Angel noticed a frown on Rudy's face. But she knew the bridegroom could not see the bride yet.

At last the time came! It was two o'clock, and everyone was seated. The minister was standing in his spotless black suit, with a prayer book in his hand. Angel had goose bumps on her arms! And then she heard her mother say, "Where is Alyce? I don't believe Alyce is here yet!"

The wedding party surely could not start down the steps in time to the music without the maid of honor! Rudy's aunt was lining everyone up — first Rags, then Angel, then a space where Alyce should be, and then their mother, looking more bridelike than ever in her new teal dress, carrying white roses with green ferns and white ribbons cascading from them.

Some very loud chords sounded on the piano, the cue for Rags to start down the stairs with his ring pillow, which was fastened with elastic around his hand. The ring was fastened to the pillow with elastic also. But Rags did not start, because Angel held him back. "We have to wait for Alyce!" she said. "We can't have a wedding without the maid of honor!"

Margaret sounded the chords once more, louder this time. What in the world had happened to Alyce? Now she would have to parade in in front of the guests, crawling over their knees to get upstairs! Even Angel knew the wedding party was supposed to be assembled beforehand.

Sure enough, just when Margaret was sounding the chords for the third time, Angel heard a commotion at the door, and loud whispering. Then a sort of bustling sound, and the words "Excuse me," "Please excuse me," as Alyce crawled around flowers, gifts, and guests. Any second now, Angel would see Alyce, perhaps overdressed in ruffles and lace. She closed her eyes. Alyce dashed up the stairs. Angel expected to hear her muttering apologies for her tardiness, but she didn't offer a one! She acted as if she did not even *know* that she had kept the whole wedding, bride and minister included, waiting!

Finally, Angel could not delay it any longer.

She had to open her eyes or she would fall down the steps. And what she saw was not a dress of ruffles and lace that outshone her mother's. It was not a fancy dress Alyce had on, or one too brightly colored. In fact, thought Angel, any of those things would be better than what she saw in front of her. For Alyce was wearing the very same dress that her mother was getting married in! The lovely teal color, the fine design, the good fit. A wonderful dress, except that the bride and the maid of honor looked like identical twins!

Angel looked at her mother, in panic. She wanted to shout, "I *told* you to shop with Alyce!" but she didn't. She was speechless. And she felt too sorry for her mother to make any comment at all. Angel's mother had the same look of horror on her face that Angel felt. Alyce, however, did not seem to notice. She just winked at Angel, and took her place in line, holding the bouquet that was thrust into her hand by a floral assistant.

Why was it, thought Angel, the things a person worries about do not happen, but out of the

blue something completely new and different oc-
curs? All her worrying about a too-frilly dress,
and about Rudy's friends arriving in clown cos-
tumes had been unnecessary. If only she had
known, she would have worried about the right
things!

Now the Wedding March had definitely begun. "Go ahead, Rags!" said their mother.
"Start down the steps slowly!"

Rags did start slowly. But what Angel's mother
had not told him was, "Walk on two feet."
Turning the pillow to the back of his hand, Rags
was crawling down the stairs on all fours, and
making some strange growling noise with his
voice. Angel, still in shock from seeing Alyce in
her mother's bridal dress, took some time to take
it all in. By the time she shouted "Stand up!" in
a loud whisper, Rags was at the bottom of the
stairs and moving into the audience.

There was nothing for Angel to do but follow.
It was bad enough having disaster ahead of her,
and behind her; she could not afford to make a

single mistake herself. When she got to the bottom of the steps and turned the corner into the living room, she could see Rags, upright now but dancing and twirling on his toes, instead of walking sedately toward the artificial fireplace.

And when Angel glanced behind her (as she turned) Alyce was smiling and waving to the guests and mouthing words to them as if she were walking down Main Street and meeting friends. Margaret Toomer played bravely on, an accompaniment to these antics. Now Rags was walking on his hands! What in the world had gotten into him, Angel wondered. Rags was not usually a bad boy. He did not deliberately set out to ruin weddings. Angel wondered if someone had cast a spell on Rags. He was acting like a perfect — *bear*!

The guests were tittering, but when Angel walked by, there were "ooohs" and "ahs" from them. "You look lovely, dear!" her new grandmother said. But no one seemed to titter *or* "oooh" and "ah" when Alyce and the bride in

their matching teal dresses came by. Maybe they
will think it was on purpose, thought Angel. Of-

ten, she knew, bridesmaids were dressed alike, if there was more than one. They may think this is a new fashion!

And then they reached the artificial fireplace, and stood in front of the minister. The music stopped, and from the dining room Rudy entered, stepped up to Angel's mother, and took her arm. He had a clean white shirt on, a lovely black tie, his face looked radiant, but — there was one thing wrong. For weeks Angel had been worrying about his friends coming in costume. Never once did she dream that Rudy would. But, standing beside his bride, the top half of him suave and sedate, Angel was aghast to see he was wearing his balloon-legged trousers with the patches on them, held up by red suspenders! Angel and her mother both knew what had happened. The cleaners had not come with his suit in time. They had not come at all!

The minister had opened his black book and was reading Scripture aloud. Everyone was looking very serious (except Rags).

"Does anyone here know of any reason why these two people should not be joined today in holy matrimony?" the minister was saying. Angel held her breath. She hoped no one stopped the wedding, which would mean it would have to be done all over again. No one said a word. The minister gave a little talk, and then Angel's mother and Rudy each said something they had composed for the occasion.

When Rudy began to talk, he put one arm around Angel's mother and the other around Angel and said how grateful he was to have a ready-made family to love. When Angel glanced up, she noticed that he had tears in his eyes. Suddenly she forgot every single worry she'd had — the look-alike dresses, Rags's antics, her new long name — and felt a great surge of love for this man who in a few moments would be her real father. She stood there in her familiar house, thinking of all the years gone by, and all of the changes that had happened. She thought of the days when she had had no friends but her mother, she thought of the dog laundry when the people had sat right here in the living room waiting for their pets! She thought of being alone when her mother was gone, of the chase down these very steps after Bubba and the mouse. And of all those

things, both good and bad, she never ever remembered being as happy as she was at this moment. Pappadopolis or not, she felt warmer than
ever toward this man who loved her, and who
made them a family — a happy family. And a
man who made her mother happy. She had
friends, a home, and now a father!

When Angel looked at her mother, she could
see in her eyes that Rudy's pants and Rags's
antics and the look-alike dresses were forgotten
by her, too. She looked happier and more at peace
than Angel had ever seen her. Her mother de-
served a honeymoon! They did need time away
together!

". . . in sickness and in health . . . till death
do you part."

"I do," said her mother and father. Angel
could hear Edna sniffling in the audience.

"And now for the ring," the minister said.

Rags was standing on the tips of his toes,
twirling, and no one tried to stop him. Rudy
simply reached out and gave the ring a tug from

its pillow, and slipped it onto Angel's mother's finger.

"With this ring," he said, "I thee wed."

And then Rudy did a surprising thing. He reached into his shirt pocket and took out a small velvet box. He opened it and turned to Angel. Right there, in the middle of her mother's wedding, Rudy placed a small gold locket around Angel's neck. On the front of the locket were engraved three letters. Angel's new initials. There was a larger P in the middle, and a small A and C on either side. She was Angel Pappadopolis from this moment on! She wanted to have Rudy's name, no matter what it was! If he had been Rudy Rhinoceros, she wouldn't have cared! Then Rudy presented Rags with a small gold watch, which had his initials on the back.

". . . I now pronounce you man and wife!" said the minister, closing his black book and reaching out to shake Rudy's hand. "Congratulations!" he said. "And now you may kiss the bride!"

At that signal, everyone clapped loudly and got to their feet and threw rice. Then they came and hugged the bridal party and, with tears in their eyes, wished them well. Those were tears of happiness, just like Angel's, she knew.

"Isn't it *romantic*?" Edna whispered into Angel's ear. "I wish I could go to *my* mother's wedding!"

"We must have shopped at the same store!" said Alyce, finally noticing that the dresses were alike.

". . . And when my suit didn't come from the cleaners, I thought I'd wear my jeans, but they had grease all over the front of them from when I changed the oil in the car for the trip," Rudy was telling someone.

When Rags explained to everyone how hard it was to be a bear without a bear suit with real fur, they finally understood. But Rags still did not understand why, if his mother wanted a ring bear, she did not expect him to look like one.

While everyone ate sandwiches, Margaret

Toomer played wedding songs on the piano, and Rudy got the dictionary and read the difference between "bear" and "bearer" to Rags, who sat on Rudy's knee eating a piece of wedding cake.

"Live and learn," Alyce called across the room to Rags.

Then the phone rang, and Rudy answered it.

"Phone call," he said, "from Kentucky. For Mrs. Pappadopolis! Is there anyone here by that name?"

Mrs. Pappadopolis came to the phone, and Angel Pappadopolis could hear Aunt Beth's voice bringing good wishes all the way from down south.

"Do you want to talk to my son and daughter, too?" called Rudy into the phone.

Daughter, thought Angel. It had been a long time since she had been a daughter to a father.

"I was a ring bear, Aunt Beth! Not a bear with fur. A bear in a suit! And Angel wouldn't be a fox.'' Rags paused. Aunt Beth must be asking questions, thought Angel.

"No, not a *bear,*" shouted Rags into the phone. Then he sighed. No one seemed to understand him. Angel knew just how he felt, but for once that didn't seem to matter a bit!